TARAM

The Generations

MAHESSWURE GURRAM

ISBN 979-8-89186-522-8

To those who never give up
on their lost loved ones in their family, like me, find it
heartbreaking
to untangle from their memories.
This book is a reminder to let you know that
Our connection with our lost family members is
immortal.
In beloved memory of
G. V. Devamma Garu and G. C. Venkataswamy Garu

CONTENTS

ACKNOWLEDGEMENTS AND A NOTE TO READERS

To My Beloved Readers,

I can't help but feel a rush of emotions surging through me as I hold this book in my hands. Writing these words and weaving this story has been a labour of love, and I am thrilled to share it with all of you.

To each reader who picks up this book, know that you hold a piece of my heart within these pages. Your curiosity and willingness to embark on this adventure mean the world to me. Thank you for giving an unknown author like me a chance, and I hope my words transport you to worlds beyond your imagination.

I am indebted to my family and friends, whose unwavering support and belief in me have been the pillars of my strength. Your encouragement and love have propelled me forward, and I am forever grateful for each of you.

Thank you to the incredible writing community for being a wellspring of inspiration and companionship. Your shared experiences and journeys have taught me valuable lessons and helped me grow as a writer—a special shout-out to my writing buddies and critique partners. Your constructive feedback and relentless enthusiasm have pushed me to be better, and I cherish the late-night brainstorming sessions and laughter-filled discussions.

To my editor and the entire publishing team, thank you for nurturing this story and turning it into a reality. Your dedication and belief in my work have made this dream come true, and I am honoured to be part of this journey with you.

I want to express my heartfelt appreciation to the bloggers, book reviewers, and bookstagrammers who have graciously embraced my book and shared their thoughts. Your words have brought tears and smiles to my eyes, and your support profoundly moves me.

I would like to extend my heartfelt gratitude to my mother, G.S. Radha Rane Garu, whose artistic talents have graced the pages of this book with a cover that is both stunning and evocative. Her dedication, creativity, and passion for art have brought my words to life in a way that words alone could never achieve.

Last but not least, to my grandmother G.V. Devamma Garu and grandfather G.C. Venkatswamy Garu, who is no longer with us but whose love and memories continue to guide me. You were my first inspiration, and I dedicate this book to your beautiful souls. Your love was my foundation, and I hope to honor your memory through my words.

To all of you, my dear readers, thank you for taking this journey with me. Your presence in my life and the world of literature fills me with boundless joy. I hope this book becomes a cherished part of your reading journey, just as it has become a precious part of mine.

With heartfelt gratitude and love,
Mahesswure Gurram

PROLOGUE

Who is God?

God is the creator of the universe and living organisms.
Okay.

Where is God, though?

They say everywhere and in everything.

But now the question arises: Why must we believe in God?

We are taught from childhood that God has a watch on us, whether we do good or bad; God is watching us, and we will have to answer to God. Why believe in God? Because he is the one with miracles and can change one's fate.

Interesting, right?

Let me ask you another question here.

We pray to God, who is the cause of our existence, but do we pray to our ancestors who hold the characteristic traits of our living?

Where have you started your life? Specifically, how did you choose your religion, caste, creed, inheritance, and characteristics?

Let me answer that for you.

We carry about 25% of our DNA from our ancestors. We hold the attributes of our ancestors in our blood, and I believe that our ancestors are a form of God.

Wait a minute. Do you still remember your ancestors?

PRESENT DAY - September 24th, 2022 (8:00 pm)

'Have you lost your mind?'

'What are you trying to do?'

'Why are you panicking when you have nothing to do with this?'

'You do not have to take this responsibility; just leave her as she is.'

'What do you think will happen now?'

All these thoughts echo while Aarav drives a car through an isolated road. The chilled breeze accompanying his cold thoughts increases the tension. Aarav shivers, not from the cold snap but from the fright tearing his insides.

His hands were cold and clammy, holding the steering; his heart pounded, his stomach clenched, his legs were wobbly with fear, and his body drenched with sweat. He jumped all at once when he heard his mobile ring. He tried to suppress his shiver when he noticed the call was from his mamá (mother).

He picked up his mobile into his hands, trying to answer the call.

'No! Don't!'

'Have you gone nuts? What will you tell your mamá (mother) if she asks you about GG?' His inner voice echoes again.

Aarav thinks about it and then puts the phone next to his seat. He tries to turn back and look at GG, who is unconscious by now with the intake of alcohol.

'It's all my fault,' mutters Aarav, grinding his teeth and gulping down his now-growing anger while looking at GG from the rear-view mirror.

An idea suddenly kicks in; the car stops while he smashes the brakes to a halt.

He quickly reaches out to his phone, surfs through his contacts, and dials Sameeksha, his hermana (Sister).

'Bro, where are you? I was about to dial your number. Tía (Aunt) was asking me about your whereabouts,' Sameeksha cries out at a stretch.

'Ay! What did you say? Did you, by any chance, mention that GG is with me?' questions Aarav with panic.

'Wait... What? Did you just say GG? Okay, now I get it, so she is with you all this while, and that's why she did not answer any of my calls,' says Sameeksha, with anger burning down her throat.

'Wow, I really can't believe her. She dumped me to spend time with you! God, I hate you, Aarav. Why did you not tell me about your plans with GG? I am not talking to either of you,' Sameeksha laughs sarcastically and continues, 'And like a fool, I am managing things here for you at home, but you people cheated on me.'

'And...' Sameeksha continues to say another word while Aarav cuts her out.

'Ushh... ShhShhShhh!! Not another word from you,' Aarav tries to increase his voice to calm Sameeksha down.

Sameeksha stays quiet for a few seconds.

'Now, hear me out. GG asked me to take her to a bar, and I denied it. After a while, I suddenly got a call from GG's phone; the bartender said GG was unstable. I picked her up from the bar, but she was unconscious by then.'

'What...?! Is GG alright?' shrikes Sameeksha into the phone almost very loudly.

'Usshh, keep your voice down. GG is alright. She is okay. She just drank too much. Now that's not a problem; How do we get her home? Yamuna abuelita (Grandma) will kill me if she gets to know I am with GG while she is drunk and passed out. And now, she will have a solid reason to stop us from meeting GG. I am terrified right now. I need you to help me through this.' Aarav pauses for a second and continues.

'Yeah, and what have you told my mamá (Mother)?' questioned Aarav.

'I told her you are at your friend's birthday party and will be home by the buffer time,' said Sameeksha.

'Uuush, gracias, a Dios. At Least she thinks I am not with GG,' says Aarav puffing out his breath.

'Don't worry; I have managed that for you. But what about GG? What do we do now?' questions Sameeksha, worried.

'I thought of an idea, which is why I called you,' said Aarav.

'What is it? What is it?' says Sameeksha, with curiosity.

'I will tell you, but before that, where is your twin?' questioned Aarav.

'Yeah, Maneeshka is at home,' said Sameeksha.

'Perfecto! Now, listen to me carefully. Ask Maneeshka to create distraction or chaos at home and get everyone's attention on her. While she does that, I want you to come to the back door and help me carry GG to her room.'

'Cool, that sounds like a plan. I will inform Maneeshka about the plan.' replies Sameeksha excitedly.

'Done. But please hurry, we are running out of time. I will have to be home by buffer time 8.30,' says Aarav with a firm voice.

'Sí Señor, do not worry about it. We will take care,' Sameeksha assured.

With quick relief, Aarav disconnects the call. Now that the clouds are slowly clearing the sky for him, Aarav hops out of the car.

He stretches his body and walks back and forth beside the vehicle. He halts near the window on the back and looks at GG.

There she is, peacefully sleeping while they struggle to save her like they always do.

He kept glaring at her for a few seconds. 'Who is this superwoman? How is she so strong for her age? Being assertive is a good thing. But he always wondered how much she had poured in or faced the rain to be this strong.'

A smile appears on Aarav's face while his thoughts are tangled. Lost in thoughts, unconsciously, he whispers, 'What is your age, GG?'

GG mutters in her past-out state, 'Fa...mi..ly..., we are a fam...' and the word suppresses under her breath.

Aarav watches her and then stands up straight, turning the other way. Frowning, he falls deeper into the pit of his thoughts, thinking about GG.

Aarav's thoughts were suddenly interrupted by a call. He shakes his head to dust out his ongoing thoughts.

He pulls out his phone from his front pocket and quickly answers it when Sameeksha's name appears on display.

'Bro, all set. Ready to go,' says Sameeksha with a chirp.

Aarav, with a smile, says, 'Cool, let's begin the game.'

AARAV

Let me start by introducing the people in our joint family. We have around four generations in our family. The fourth generation is where I come from; let me refer to my age group as G4. The head of our family, i.e., people who are part of G1, are: GG and Great-Grandpa. GG's name is "Ganga," which we later turned into GG, a short form of Great Grandma. GG's husband, Mahendra Varma, our Great-Grandpa, passed away in 2020 from a chronic heart attack after learning that a bank had taken over our ancestral house. It was a tragic loss for everyone in the family. We not only lost our family head but also our relationship with our home ended.

Our Great-Grandpa was a wonderful person with reasonable cultural beliefs and always respected all family member's suggestions and decisions. Likewise, we also value and respect household traditions. But ever since the news rang a bell about a bank taking possession of our house. That is when everything gradually changed: our house, traditions, rituals and an essential aspect, our family head.

From childhood, all I remember in our joint family is when I grew up near GG and played with my twin hermanas (Sisters) from G4. I do not have a personal connection with anyone in our family except GG and my twin hermanas

(Sisters). When I was seven, I had to move to Canada with my parents. I regret not being around during this inevitable phase of our family. We came to India permanently right after my Great-Grandpa passed away.

While our family was devastated by the loss of our family head and house, Yamuna abuelita (Grandma) took all of us in and sheltered us. Yamuna abuelita (Grandma) comes from G2. Regarding G2, GG and my Great-Grandpa have two children, one elder, hijo (Son), Rajeev Varma, and only hija (Daughter), Yamuna. For our G4, Rajeev Varma is an Abuelo (Grandpa), and Yamuna is abuelita (Grandma). After our Great-Grandpa left us, Yamuna, our abuelita, gave shelter and took control of the entire family. She is extremely strict; she always has things organised and expects our family members to be very systematic. She has also passed on a few rules and regulations the entire family should follow, with no exceptions.

On the other hand, Rajeev Varma abuelo (Grandpa) is such a sweetheart. After GG, we love Rajeev Varma abuelo (Grandpa) a lot. He takes diligent care of GG and prepares tasty food, especially pickles and snacks. Unlike Yamuna abuelita (Grandma), her hermano (Brother), our abuelo (Grandpa) is more like old school. Not that I am complaining, but he is orthodox.

Rajeev Varma abuelo (Grandpa) has only one hijo (Son), my papá (Father). My papá's (Father's) name is Raghav Varma, and he belongs to G3. Yamuna abuelita's (Grandma's) children enlarge this G3. Yamuna abuelita (Grandma) has a hija (Daughter) and a hijo (Son), Geetha tía (Aunt) and Gopal tío (Uncle). Geetha tía (Aunt) is unmarried, while Gopal tío (Uncle) is married. So, the people who belong to G3 are Raghav- my papá (Father), Gopal tío (Uncle), and

Geetha tía (Aunt)- Rajeev Varma abuelo´s (Grandpa's) and Yamuna abuelita´s (Grandma) children.

My papá (Father) Raghav Varma was married to my mamá (Mother) Gayathri (Mother) in 1997. I kick-started G4 and became a part of the family in 2003. On the other hand, Yamuna abuelita´s (Grandma's) son, Gopal tío, was married to Meenakshi tía in 1999. Sameeksha and Maneeshka joined G4 in 2004. I grew up along with my little hermanas (Sisters). I still remember playing with them in my childhood, and they are more like my best friends with whom I spend time together the most, along with GG. As the girls were just a year younger than me, I was responsible for caring for them, which I loved doing. Now that we are grown, I am sometimes bossy with them, but I often pamper them a lot. I love spending time with both my little hermanas; we three are partners in crime. Things were always smooth and fun with Sameeksha and Maneeshka until I moved to Canada with my parents.

Later, after three years, we had a new entry into our G4. The twin hermanas (Sisters) got a younger hermano (Brother) in 2007. Dhruv is a very pampered kid, the youngest of the family and the last person in G4. Sameeksha, Maneeshka and I still remember how excited we were to meet him when he was born. We were delighted to have a cute baby hermano (Brother) in our G4. But now, he has turned out to be the naughtiest of all, and we keep a watch on him as he can quickly drive us into any pit and make us stand guilty in front of our Yamuna abuelita (Grandma).

Everyone in the family fears Yamuna abuelita (Grandma) as she leads the house, placing everyone in the discipline. Abuelita (Grandma) wants us to be responsible and punishes people who commit big or small mistakes.

It goes by this saying, 'Admitting a mistake does not make things right; a mistake is always a mistake. Either big or small, you cannot undo it.'

Here are a few family rules we follow: everyone must have food together, i.e., breakfast and dinner. During this time, strictly no talking, no phones, and one should maintain pin-drop silence. Dinner is sometimes an exception, but having breakfast together is necessary. Breakfast starts at 8:30 a.m. sharp. To date, no one has ever come late for breakfast. Our food is also measured so that we do not overeat. Though having dinner together is an exception, if anyone misses it, they should write an explanation in the "Book of Rules" as to why they did not attend family dinner. Also, this strict rule applies only to G4; we should return home by 8:00 p.m.; If we are running late, the buffer time is 8:30 p.m. because dinner starts at 8:30 sharp. If we cross the buffer time, punishment follows. The penalties which we have in place are insane, is what I feel. We will be assigned a few chores for three days during our sentence. Also, we are not allowed to hang out with GG. And most importantly, family dinner is not an exception for punished people.

There was a time when I was way too late to return home as I went to watch a movie with my friends. I showed up at home around 8:40 p.m., which is fair enough. But, my abuelita (Grandma) asked me for an explanation, and she did not consider my answer reasonable. After which, I had to do chores for three days and always made sure I headed home directly after college. There was no hanging out with GG, hermanas (Sisters) and not with my amigos (friends). The worst part of this punishment was having mandatory family dinners. On the third day of my sentence, I was tired and frustrated with the daily chores. I was unable to bear the loud silence in the dining hall, so I happened to use my phone secretly, which made things worse for me. I was scrolling through Instagram feeds under the table, giggling at memes.

I was just trying to cheer myself up from the long day. But, to my bad luck, one of the memes produced loud music, to which everyone jumped at once in their seats, including me. And later, I had to dance to the music my abuelita (Grandma) played. My punishment was extended for another week, for which Sameeksha, Maneeshka and GG continued to make fun of me to date.

The bond I share with GG and my sisters is an overwhelming force that fills my heart with love, joy, and a deep sense of connection. It is a bond that transcends generations, draped knit with threads of shared memories, laughter, and cherished moments.

Our GG, with her wisdom and gentle spirit, holds a special place in my heart. Her presence is a light of strength and resilience, a living proof of the passage of time and the richness of life's experiences. Every interaction with her feels like a treasure as I absorb her stories and teachings, knowing they are a precious gift that will shape my journey.

In the embrace of my sisters, I find solace and companionship. They are my confidantes, my partners in laughter and tears, and my unwavering support system. With each other, we navigate the twists and turns of life, knowing that an unbreakable bond binds us.

The overwhelming feeling that washes over me when we are together is a mixture of gratitude, comfort, and a profound sense of belonging. The invisible thread that weaves us together draws us closer with each passing day.

In our moments of shared laughter, the room comes alive with contagious joy. We create memories that will be etched in our hearts forever, building a tapestry of experiences that will shape our lives and leave an indelible mark on our souls.

During hardship, our bond strengthens, offering unwavering support and heaven for vulnerability. We stand shoulder to shoulder, weathering life's storms with resilience and knowing we are never alone.

The overwhelming love I feel for my great-grandmother and sisters extends beyond words. It is a bond that transcends distance and time, reminding me of the power of family and its profound impact on shaping who we are.

In embracing this bond, I find a sense of grounding and purpose. It fuels my aspirations, encourages me to be the best version of myself, and reminds me of the legacy that we carry forward as a family.

Reflecting on this bond's overwhelming nature, I am grateful for our shared moments and the love that binds us. It is a reminder that no matter where life takes us, the strength of our connection will always endure, providing a sanctuary of love and support in a world that can often feel chaotic.

With each passing day, I treasure the moments we spend together, knowing they are a testament to the power of family and the extraordinary bond that ties us all together. It is a bond that transcends time and space, reminding me that I am truly blessed to have such an overwhelming love in my life.

SAMEEKSHA

GG has always been this trendy, cool, fun-loving, up-front Great-Grandma anyone would envy her for her intelligence and humour nature at this age of hers. Not just me, my siblings, Maneeshka and Aarav, everyone is proud of her. She is not just our Great-Grandma but also our best friend; we always look up to her more than our parents. But sadly, we do not like how our family members treat her. She has got all that respect, but no one gives an ear to her. What is the aspect of respecting someone when they are unheard of? What kind of respect is that? After our Great-Grandpa left us, GG was never the same; the family has never treated her the same. GG's hija (Daughter) Yamuna- technically, our Abuelita (Grandma) has taken over the family's possessions and disciplined the family under her roof. Though it is not openly said, it is evident that our Abuelita (Grandma) had some issues with her parents, i.e., GG and Great-Grandpa, of which the three of us are unaware.

GG and I share a very thick bond; we do all the girly things together, from gossiping to nail painting. No doubt Aarav gets good attention being the eldest bisnieto (Great-Grandson). However, I, on the other hand, as a bisnieta (Great-Granddaughter), get that special attention from GG. Not just me; even my twin Maneeshka receives the same special attention as mine. There is this saying, 'Birds with the same feathers flock together', and that's how we girls are; GG, Maneeshka and I gel well together.

Maneeksha is my twin and is just 1 minute younger than me, but we are remarkably similar. We both are the first bisnieta (Great-granddaughters) in the family. Though Aarav, our cousin hermano (brother), is a year older than Maneeshka and I, it goes without saying that girls bring in the rays of sunshine to a family.

In our joint family, our fourth generation started with Aarav. Maneeshka and I are remarkably close to Aarav, as he is just a year older than us. While we both are 18, Aarav is 19, which brings a slight difference between us.

We share everything and support each other when there is any issue. Aarav is a chill person; however, he holds vast responsibilities. He is solid and has clear thoughts, especially regarding GG. We three love GG and spend decent quality time with her the most. We share many memories with GG. Maneeshka and I also have a naughty yet annoying, younger teenage hermano (Brother) who does not hold any of our secrets, especially GG-related ones.

Dhruv is a mamá's (Mother's) pet and a secret investigation officer whose duty is always to dig a graveyard pit for Aarav, Maneeshka and me. In simple words, he pours in fuel to the happening fire. Dhruv is three years younger than us and does not understand or even try to understand the reasons or our purposes. He is 15 years old but will soon be 16 years old this December. He is very pampered as he is the youngest within our whole family and the last person of our 4th generation.

At that very moment, while we were planning a rescue mission for GG, I could only think about Dhruv. If Dhruv learns about our plan or messes up our game plan, we will get kicked from a cliff into a burning volcano. After reciting the situation to Maneeshka, who is now walking back and forth inside the room, scratching her head for an idea. I started giving work to my brain. I suddenly jump out of my bed and walk towards Maneeshka while Maneeshka stops at a place.

'Mannu, Mannu, listen… I have an idea,' I say, pulling Maneeshka by her hand and making her sit with me at the bedside. I fold my legs up and sit comfortably to shoot my plan.

'Yeah, what is it?' questions Maneeksha, with curiosity in her eyes.

'So, here is the thing… You remember you said you wanted to go on an excursion with your college friends?'

'Sí, what about it? But let us talk about that later. First, we will figure out how to get Aarav and GG out of this trouble. Focus, Sameeksha.'

I frown, holding my head and say, 'Ay! Mannu, that is the plan.' Maneeshka looks at me with a question-mark expression. I pull her closer to me and try to whisper.

'Okay, listen carefully… You will be creating a distraction by trying to sneak away from home for the excursion trip with your friends,' I whisper to her in a low tone.

As I say this, her eyes are bright with joy. Even though she has not expressed it in words, I can already sense her excitement. She almost tries to open her mouth to show her excitement, but I close her mouth with my hands and say, 'Shh… shh… We must be careful; Dhruv should not get a hint about this,'

She nods, and then I remove my hands from her mouth.

'Sam, how do we gather everyone? You know what I mean, right? This should not be like; we are doing it on purpose,' says Maneeshka, looking into my eyes.

I got what she was saying. Everything should be natural. It should not be like we are acting. We both looked at each other for a few seconds. Now, it was Maneeshka's turn to jump up with an idea.

Maneeshka whisperingly says, 'We can trick Dhruv into this,' and lets out a smirk which soon turns to a laugh. I join her with a laugh, and we raise our hands to hi-five.

We all know Dhruv can never hold on to a secret, especially if it is our secret. He will surely dump it into our mamá's (Mother's) ears. This idea excited Maneeshka and me.

'So, how are we doing this then?' I questioned Maneeshka.

Her smile widens as she clears her throat and whispers again, 'So, I will speak on the phone with my friend and pack my luggage. I will make sure Dhruv listens to my conversation. While he gets this to mamá (Mother), I will be nearing the living area,' We both exchange broad smiles. I pull Maneeshka into a quick hug.

'Alright then, let's start with it; we are running out of time.' I say.

'Sí, let's get started. I will check on Dhruv,' says Maneeshka, jumping out of bed and heading straight to the door.

I pull out my phone, dial Aarav, and tell him about the update so he can head home. Once everything is precise, I will signal him and fetch GG from the backdoor.

We faced many situations, but we never had a complex problem that we are encountering right now. It's not about

GG consuming alcohol or passing out. It's about our abuelita (Grandma), i.e., Yamuna GG's hija (Daughter); she already gave all three of us a last warning about how selflessly we are spending time with GG and how GG is selflessly taking advantage of that with the increase in time. According to Yamuna abulieta (Grandma), we have one last chance with her, and if she finds us hanging out with GG, she will confront GG and ground us from meeting her.

That has made all three of us worrisome.

3

MANEESHKA

'No, I am just waiting for clearance in the living room. I will sneak out at a perfect time,' I say over the phone, a little louder, making sure to get Dhruv's attention.

I stand facing the window to observe Dhruv's movements reflecting on the window glass. I see him capping the water bottle while he takes teeny-tiny steps towards me to make sure what he is eavesdropping on.

'Do not worry; I have packed my luggage. I can't miss this chance to attend the excursion trip with my dearest friends,' I say with a little exaggeration.

That triggered the fire, and I could see him moving back and forth, not knowing what action he needed to take.

I quickly turned around to face him, to which he was caught off-guard and started looking away. And I, on the other hand, began acting as if I was caught off-guard and continued talking over the phone.

'Ha..ha... Ah, ya, ya. We will have to submit the assignment by this week. Don't worry; we will work on this together,' I say over the phone.

I smile at Dhruv, and he smiles back with a weird expression. Right at that moment, I understood what was running through his mind. I pull his cheeks while I continue to talk over the phone.

'Okay, we will catch up soon. Bye!' I giggled before disconnecting the call.

'Who was it, Mannu?' questions Dhruv with a firm voice.

'Mi amiga.' I shrug while I say.

Dhruv raises his eyebrows and looks at me seriously. I start acting as if I am nervous, scratching behind my ear and letting out a weird laugh. That's what I do when I am scared, and Dhruv knows it.

'You look nervous. What are you up to, Mannu?' he questions me with a rugged look and notices my suitcase on the bed. 'And, what is that for? Where are you heading?' Dhruv points at the suitcase.

I let out a nervous laugh once again 'lol, why will I be nervous,' I say and scratch behind my ear again. 'That.. oh... You mean the suitcase,' I laughed nervously, 'Sí, right. I was organising my wardrobe. Don't mind that,' I shrugged and waved my hand.

He smirks at me and laughs, 'Alright then, I have a quick meeting with Mum. Bye, see you around.' he walks towards the door.

'Wipe that bloody smirk out of your face Dhruv,' I try to yell at him to pump up the situation.

I cross my arms and stand right where he left me.

He turns back, looks at me sharply, and gestures, mouthing the words, 'I am watching you.' After which, he walks out of the door in haste.

As soon as he leaves the room, I quickly pull out my phone and post this update on our WhatsApp group for Aarav and Sameeksha to read.

I quickly grab my suitcase and rush to the living room. I wait in the living room to get caught by someone.

I suddenly hear footsteps approaching, so I position myself at the entrance to open the front door.

I jerk when I hear Dhruv shouting and asking mamá (Mother) to hurry up. 'Mum, look, I caught her. She is heading out.'

Mamá (Mother) approaches behind Dhruv, looks at my suitcase and says, 'What is happening, Mannu? Where are you going at this time?'

I open my mouth to start a conversation, and Dhruv cuts me off and starts to complain.

'Mum, I told you right! Mannu is going on an excursion trip with her friends, and here you spot her with her luggage, trying to sneak out! Trust me, Mum! I am never wrong.'

Dhruv folds his arms and repeatedly strikes another smirk. I glare at him for a good long second.

'Mannu! Is Dhruv right?! Answer me?!' questions mamá (Mother) with an enraged tone. I can sense the tension on her face, a wrinkle on her forehead, and her eyebrows almost twitching.

I lower my head and stay quiet.

'I need an answer, Mannu. Talk to me!' mamá (Mother) yells.

With her yelling at me, she grabbed the entire family's attention and slowly, people started coming to see the show I put on.

I see my papá's (Father's) hermana (Sister) Geetha tía (Aunt) walking towards the living room with a confused expression. On the other side, I notice Rajeev Varma abuelo (Grandpa) and Dakshayani abuelita (Grandma) holding hands, walking towards the living area, and taking seats on the sofa to watch my drama.

Also, I hear Aarav's mamá (Mother), Gayathri tía (Aunt), who is in the kitchen, yelling, enquiring about what is happening in the living area.

Now, I know that my plan is working out. I feel very excited and happy. But, at that very moment, I was also a little scared about how I would face Yamuna abuelita (Grandma) if she suddenly showed up.

'Look at her; she is sneaking out somewhere. I did not believe it when Dhruv told me until I saw her with this suitcase, preparing to leave,' said mamá (Mother) with a worried tone.

My papá (Father) Gopal was in utter shock; he walked towards me and tried to lift my head which was facing my feet until then. I try not to look at him, but he looks right into my eyes and says, 'Look at the clock; it's 8:15 pm, almost dinner time. Will you stay quiet until Yamuna abuelita (Grandma) comes and questions you, or will you explain to us and get it done right here,'

I look at my papá (Father) with terror and then try to look at the Apple watch on my wrist. 'Ay, Dios mío, Sí! It is 8:15 p.m., and 8:30 is dinner time.' I think to myself.

I need to buy more time, I think to myself. While I looked at the watch, suddenly, a message popped up; it was from Aarav. I tap on the wristwatch to read the text message, "@Sam: I'm here; come to the backdoor", reads the text message.

I look at the text message and then at my papá (Father). I keep switching back and forth from text messages to my papá, From my papá (Father) to the message I received. I do it 3-4 times now. After which, I fixed my eye contact on my papá (Father), made a frown and began my crocodile tears to buy the time I wanted.

My papá (Father) looks at me and rolls his eyes, saying, 'Not again! We all know your little drama.'

I try to cry even more loudly, and while I do that, I see Sameeksha heading towards the backdoor slowly. Seeing me cry, Dakshyani abuelita (Grandma) walks up and says, 'Ay mi pobre bebe, don't cry. It's okay. You don't have to tell them. Tell your Abuelita what happened. Won't you tell your Abuelita (Grandma)?'

I nod my head in agreement and hug her. Now that everyone is paying attention, I begin to make up a story.

'So.. there is this trend going on in Instagram… we will have to throw the suitcase on the front porch .. And.. then… from the porch, the suitcase will be turned into me with the fashionable clothes I have..' I cough and take a few gulps of air in between.

As soon as I stop, I get an instant reaction from Dhruv 'Ay, Dios mío! She is lying! I heard her talking about sneaking out with her friend over the phone,'

Dhruv almost yells, his face now turned into a tomato from shouting.

At this very moment, I notice Aarav, Sameeksha and GG entering from the backdoor. So, I try to grab more of Dhruv's attention and heat things for him so that he falls right into my pit.

'Come on, Dhruv, don't make up stories. And I am going to prove you wrong, this time at any cost,' I say, almost hugging my suitcase.

I know how my little hermano's (Brother's) brain works. I purposefully clutched the suitcase to make him think I was possessive about it, which indirectly meant I hid something in it.

As I embraced the suitcase, I noticed him looking at it. He comes closer to me and grabs my suitcase. I hold on to it very tightly now.

'Mum, she is hiding something in it. Look, she is not letting me touch it,' Dhruv yells while grabbing the suitcase from me.

'Don't you have manners, Dhruv? I am not hiding anything. I am not letting you touch my things. Leave my suitcase right away. Mamá (Mother), tell him to let go of it.'

'No, I am never wrong. Why are you stressing so much if you have nothing to hide? Open up the damn suitcase and show it to everyone here.'

We keep pulling the suitcase from both ends. I try to put my upper body weight on the suitcase as I pull it towards me.

'Enough, both of you. Stop it!' says mamá (Mother) with a heated voice now.

'It's 8:25 already; your Yamuna Abuelita will be here in 5 mins for dinner. If you keep fighting like this, you must face the music. Give me the suitcase right away,' says mamá (Mother).

Dhruv, and I quickly got up and moved away from the suitcase. While Mamá (Mother) walks closer to it.

'Mamá (Mother), I am sorry for this. Go ahead and check my suitcase, you will find all fashionable dresses, from pretty gowns to festive wear. If I am sneaking out, why will I carry all these? Instead, I would have taken casual wear,' I say apologetically.

Mamá (Mother), with her crossed arms, keeps glaring at both of us with her eyebrows raised. She bends down in front of the suitcase to open it. And there, she finds all the festive clothes. Now that things are clear, everyone's eyes are stuck on Dhruv.

'No.. she… she did something. I swear, Mum. I heard her speak on the phone,' says Dhruv, almost shocked.

'Dhruv, you should come out of this bad habit of eavesdropping and pranking, see… You have wasted everyone's time here. I am just giving you friendly advice, that's it,' I say, patting his shoulders.

Dhruv is still in shock. He did not expect this twist in the story and was unprepared for it. I turn around to see everyone's reaction. My face was bright when I noticed Aarav and Sameeeksha slowly camouflaged among the group, but I tried not to smile at them.

Sameeksha winks at me while Aarav gives a thumbs-up.

A voice from the kitchen grabs everyone's attention, 'Dinner is ready, kids help me set up the table,' says Gayathri tía (Aunt).

While everyone starts to disperse, Yamuna abuelita (Grandma) emerges from her room and walks down the stairs. She notices everyone in the living area and says, 'What are we gathered here for?'

Everyone speaks in unison, "Nothing". After which, my papá continues, "It's dinner time, right, so everyone is heading to the dining. Come on, everyone, make your way to the dining hall,'

I breathe out a sigh of relief and wait while everyone leaves to join Aarav and Sameeksha. I give a quick fist bump to both of them and pull them into a side hug.

It was good to have everyone at the dinner after a long time except GG. What a day it was. All I can think about is GG while I dig into my meal.

GG

NEW MOON DAY - September 25th, 2022 (3.00 PM)
'Darkness... Darkness, Darkness..'

I open my eyes to darkness. 'Why is it pitch dark in here? And why is the house so silent?' I start to think while I rub my eyes to get a better view, but it's still dark.

I close my eyes and shake my head rapidly to become sober immediately and anticipate my headache evaporating. I opened my eyes, expecting to see some light in my room, but it was still the same, coal black. I breathe a sigh of strain in my nerves and leave the bed.

I take baby steps to ensure I do not trip and break my bones in this unlit environment. While I slid slowly towards my room entrance, I suddenly saw a flash of light between the door sill's gap. That light was indeed very radiant; my calculations typically nearing the maximum light intensity that a human eye can take.. 'Approximately 1200 nanometers' at that moment, I felt lucky that the door was in between, blocking the light from reaching my old optic vision.

I brace myself up, and near the door, I hear a faint voice that is very familiar. I tried to eavesdrop on what the voice was saying. 'No! Not this time,' an elderly male voice says, almost breaking down.

'I recognise that voice… it's… it's my husband!! Mahendra Varma!!' I say while I pull open the door knob in haste. As I open the door, the voice becomes soft, distancing away. I step out of the room to follow the voice. I was amazed by my view as I stepped into a different place similar to our house, except it was warmer, brighter, and everything was high-tech. It's more like a future world. Observing the advancement around me, I keep walking towards the living room.

My eyes were curious in the hope of catching sight of my husband, and my ears were craving that calming yet firm voice, and my heart was optimistic about spending the time with him which was once lost.

'Ganga,' calls out a soft voice from behind me.

I turn around to see my husband beaming in that gleam. He was the kind of good-looking that got into my bones, that spoke to me of olden times before he'd said a word. I was amused by the stunning personality that he had. But something was different about him; he seemed younger than me and had one strike mark across his forehead. He was not happy, but the brightness on his face did not divert me from the sadness in his eyes.

'I… uh.. I. Ahem, I,' my words keep stuttering all of a sudden. I gasp a bit and gulp down some air.

'Ganga, It's you!' says Mahendra Varma.

I moved closer to my husband to hold his hands, but for some reason, I could not grasp his hands, 'Sí, it's me! It's your Ganga,' I say with my head down while tears glide down my cheeks.

Suddenly, without any notice, this darkened dullness starts to consume the illuminating flash of ignite like a shadow swallowing the light. This dark fogginess has begun rising from the ground towards an upward direction.

There was an unknown fear apart from the sadness that was dancing in my husband's eyes. He looked me eye to eye and said, 'You need to save our family, keep us alive. We are running out of time…' he stops briefly, with a sudden terrified look on his face and says …. 'he is coming.'

I felt the stress filling the atmosphere; I questioned Mahendra Varma, 'He? Who is he?' I enquire with a firm tone.

'Danger. Our family,' He says and evaporates into thin air.

'No! No! Don't go,' I let out a cry.

I touched the place where my husband was standing seconds ago. As he whooshed away, the radiance lingered around him, gobbled by jet darkness all over the house. I felt the emptiness surrounding me, drowning me in a darker pit. I go deeper and deeper into this black hole. My mind is wobbling with mixed emotions and thoughts, but even in this chaos, my inner soul awaits to seek my husband's hand, who would have pulled me out of this echoing darkness by now. But there is no sign of him.

I wrestle myself from holding myself back, giving up on myself, and keeping myself suffocated. I struggle to breathe, and my hands automatically search for things around me to get a hold of something. Suddenly I snapped out of the gloomy torment as I felt a touch that grabbed my hand and pulled me out of the darkness. I open my eyes to a fuzzy view of 3 silhouettes watching me closely. I quickly pull my hand from that grip and buff my eyes off for a better sight.

'Calm down, GG!...' says Sameeksha.

'GG, we are right here with you,' Aarav speaks with a calming voice.

'It must have been a nightmare. But that's ok. You are fine,' says Maneeksha with an assuring tone.

At once, I see them. My children. My great-grandchildren. I grab the three of them into a hug.

'It's okay, GG, it was just a nightmare. We are right here for you,' says Aarav.

I nod in agreement and pull away from the hug. "What time is it?" I asked them.

'It's 3 p.m.; we just had our lunch and came to check on you,' said Sameeksha looking at me.

'GG, why don't you freshen up and eat something? You were knocked out for so many hours. Aren't you hungry? What was that dream about? You still look freaked out. Why don't you….' Maneeksha speaks out at a stretch while Sameeksha cuts her out as she thumps Maneeksha on the head.

'That's enough, Mannu. Let's give GG some time to freshen up first,' says Sameeksha looking at Maneeskha and Aarav.

'Yeah, come on girls, let's head out,' says Aarav and starts to move towards the door. Aarav heads out, followed by Sameeksha and Maneeshka. The three of them walk away in a queue.

I sit there for an adequate amount of time while the dream keeps running back in my mind. It was not just a dream; it was more than a dream. It was a feeling; it was more like a real-world experience.

My inner voice keeps yelling, 'You need to speed up your hunt for the laud key; you are running out of time.

But... But... Danger to our family? Who is coming? Is there any threat?'

I firmly made up my mind not to waste any further time. I quickly leave the bed and head into the washroom to freshen up.

* * *

'Shh... Ushh! Keep your voice low, Mannu,' says Sameeksha with fright.

'Sí, we all know that today is the day for Yamuna abuelita's (Grandma's) weird, obscured act. Nevertheless, I always wonder what is in that room. Why does Yamuna abuelita (Grandma) spend time in that locked room every other new moon day? And most importantly, Why is no one allowed in that room, and what is she hiding from everyone?' says Sameeksha in a more bottomless shaft of thoughts.

'Girls, let's do something crazy tonight then, shall we?' says Aarav with a smirk.

Immediately the girls look at each other in disbelief and look back at Aarav when Maneeksha says, 'Bro, are you suggesting that we must find out Yamuna abuelita's (Grandma's) little secret?'

'You never know if it's a little one or a huge one until we find out about the mystery,' says Aarav with a wink.

'Hell no, if we get caught by anyone or Yammuna abuelita (Grandma), for that matter of fact, we will be departed to heaven all at once,' says Sameeksha seriously. 'But it's worth trying,' smiles Sameeksha and lets out a wink.

The three of them laugh in unison.

'Did I miss out on something? What are the waves of laughter all about?' I chuckle as I join their club at the dining table.

'GG! You are right on time. Come, we will serve you lunch,' says Maneeksha.

I nod and take an empty seat at the centre of the table. All three gather around me and start to serve food items individually, taking turns. The affection they show is no less than a mamá (Mother) pampering her child who sulks without eating. I always feel so blessed to meet and make memories with this pack of generations while I am still alive. Their unconditional love towards me brought out the best in me.

After my husband Mahendra Varma left me, a part of me died the same day. Still, I've gathered myself up and stayed strong for my children. But little did I know that my children were one step ahead of me and were much stronger than I thought. It's good to be emotionally strong when you lose loved ones, but being emotionally strong to take advantage of an old widowed mamá (Mother) was heartbreaking.

That's when I started noticing the true colours of my children. I always needed clarification on why age affects relationships or how people get treated when they are aged. Being old is not a crime; one fine day, every human being on earth ages, and at that time, all they desire is some love, care, company and, most importantly, the respect given once before they aged.

Nevertheless, I feel fortunate to have learnt about each person in my family before things went out of hand. The love I get from my great-grandchildren is without any limitations to it, and I enjoy their company the most. I have grown up in their generation, and they always keep saving me. My great-grandchildren are the dots that connect the lines from generation to generation; they never belittled me, neither my age nor my love.

I quickly finish my lunch and notice the time is nearing 5 pm, so I try to head out in search of the laud key; that's when Yamunna, my hija (Daughter), stops me from stepping out.

'Mamá (Mother), you know you cannot leave my house on a new moon day. Don´t you?' says Yamuna with a firm questioning voice.

'Right, it's your house. But it's my will to head out. I don't need your permission,' I growl.

'Well, as it is the new moon today, you have to take my permission,' says Yamuna with a solid commanding tone.

Everyone in the house starts to gather in the living room, hearing our heated-up disagreements to check on who the ill-fated person to get bashed up by Yamuna is.

'Why? What is it on a new moon day, and why are you so particular about it?' I inquired with a suspicious yet curious tone.

'That is none of your concern. All you are worried about is drinking and getting wasted,' says Yamuna carelessly.

'That explains how much you know about your mamá (Mother). But that is not what I am heading out for. I have unfinished business. I need to locate the laud key.' I say, lost in thoughts.

'Come on, mamá (Mother). I have already warned you to stop looking for it. Leave the past in the past; there's no way for us to practise or celebrate the Day of the Dead festival in this house, in my house.' yells Yumana and gets back into her room angrily.

I stand there with a heavy heart and utter shock. I looked at my family members, who surrounded me; no one spoke. Everyone stood their ground with a sympathetic look on their faces.

My great-grandchildren came running to me and took me to my room. All of us sit there in silence until Maneeshka breaks the ice. 'GG, do you mind if I ask you something?'

I simply nod in agreement.

'What is wrong between you and Yamunna Abulieta? What is the key that you are looking for? And what is the story behind New Moon Day and the locked room?'

'I have no clue about the new moon day or what happens in the locked room. But, in order for you to know about the laud key, you first need to know about our family history and the traditional gift passed to us from generation to generation,' I say.

YAMUNA

Memories are one of the most crucial things we can cherish. They can be both good and bad but still impact one's life. And one of the most precious memories one can recall is childhood memories. The things a person learns during childhood remain important lessons and memories for life. It applies to things like family and society values, morals, understanding the importance of friendships and being respectful to adults. I had a beautiful childhood, and in those delightful days, all my memories were filled with Narendra Varma tío (Uncle).

Narendra Varma tío (Uncle) is my papá's (Father's) hermano (Brother), and he was the first person to take me into his arms when I was born. Tío (Uncle) was more than anyone to me; he was my best friend. I spent most of my quality time with tío (Uncle). I grew closer to him as he raised me through thick and thin. He is protective, caring, and has a powerful sense of humour. If anyone was a clone of how I thought, it is my tío (Uncle); he has a mind like mine. We have an excellent understanding; we keep each other's secrets.

I spent 18 years around him; he was my only strength. Unfortunately, we lost him to a tragic car accident. Grief arrived like a severe storm, non-stop and unforgiving.

It swallowed me whole like a sinking ship dragged into the depths of an abyss. Each day became an endless desert, where tears fell like scattered grains of sand, crumbling my spirit.

Losing him was similar to a symphony silenced, the melody abruptly cut off, leaving only an empty echo that reverberated through my soul. The world turned monochrome as if all colours had drained from existence, and I found myself wandering through a grayscale reality.

He was like a lighthouse that guided my way, but now I stumble in darkness, searching for the flicker of his light. The void he left behind is an unfillable pit, a black hole that consumes my every thought, pulling me further into despair.

It feels like a part of me has shattered. The pieces punctured my heart, a constant reminder of what was lost, leaving behind an ache that filled my existence.

The sorrow of losing him is like an ancient oak tree stripped of its vibrant leaves standing in the harsh winter winds. It is a haunting melody that lingers, an unfinished poem with words never written.

I am adrift in a sea of memories, clinging to pieces of the past like driftwood, desperately trying to keep his essence alive. But with each passing day, the waves of sorrow crash against my fragile defences, wearing them down until I am left exposed, raw, and vulnerable.

The ache of his absence is a constant companion, a heavy cloak I wear, weighing me down with the weight of what could have been. A moment of loss suspends me, longing for his presence and mourning my loss.

The void he left behind is a wound that will forever bleed, a scar that will never heal. The sorrow of losing him is a bittersweet symphony, where the echoes of his memory tangle with the ache of his absence, creating a melody of longing that vibrates through the chambers of my heart.

During that phase, I never thought that when you lose someone you love, it feels like your heart has been ripped from your chest as you will never smile again, the sun will never shine again, and you will never know a moment of happiness again. It feels like someone turned off the sun, and there is only darkness to fumble around.

It is devastating, earth-shaking, heartbreaking, and life-altering. The only comfort in grief is that it comes in waves. When you feel you are going to drown from the weight of it, it pulls away and gives you respite. Then, out of the blue, a thought, a song, a smell, a memory grabs hold of your heart, and the waves pour over you again.

It is devastating and leaves an ache in your heart that will never heal. It is the most profound pain any human being can endure. We survive because we must, but we are forever changed. That is how it feels to lose someone you love.

I was never the same after I lost him. This disaster was unquestionably generated. A traumatic condition for me, and I struggled. To add to my misery, my parents set up my marriage with one of my papá's (Father's) close friend's sons right in that year. I was never in my right mind since tío (Uncle) left us; my parents simply led my life, and I could do nothing about it. My parents believed and considered it auspicious to conduct the marriage of a close family member within a year of the death of a person in the family.

My heart was heavy with a mix of emotions, including resentment and anger, as I battled with the decision made by my family to arrange my marriage within a relatively short time after the loss of my beloved tío. The pain I felt from the loss was still raw and consuming, and the thought of moving forward so quickly felt like an overwhelming betrayal.

In my grief-stricken state, I couldn't understand how my family, who should have been aware of my emotional turmoil, could make such a decision without considering my mental well-being. The weight of the loss still lingered within me, and the idea of entering into a new phase of life felt like an imposition, a disregard for my feelings.

The sense of anger and resentment towards my family began to build as I questioned their motives and their understanding of my needs. It felt like they were more focused on societal expectations and fulfilling traditional obligations rather than considering my emotional state and granting me the time and space to heal.

I have experienced a deep sense of betrayal, as though my family failed to comprehend the depth of my pain and the need for a slower, more compassionate approach. The hasty decision to arrange my marriage without considering my grief left me feeling isolated and misunderstood.

Amidst these overwhelming emotions, I have also struggled with a sense of powerlessness. It can be incredibly disempowering when our desires and emotional needs are disregarded, leaving us feeling voiceless and trapped in circumstances that do not align with our sense of healing and readiness.

Apart from this terrible loss, I hated that my family did not step into my shoes and feel my emotions or how hopeless I felt. They would not have arranged my marriage in my grief if they knew how I felt. It felt like I was trapped within my mind with memories filled with the times I spent with my tío.

I was just 18 years old and grieving over losing my beloved, but my family only cared about my marriage. At that very moment, I started hating my family - My mamá (Mother), my papá (Father), and my hermano (Brother).

They did not respect my feelings or value my consent to marry. Why is a girl subjected to such brutal situations of decisions and cornered to a wall? In the first place, my family never understood me; they never understood what I was going through. They never cared for me. They never knew how my mental condition was; if they ever knew any of this, they would have never taken such a decision while I was sore from the wounds.

I felt very lonely; I was broken not because of my loss but also because of my family. They deserted me by getting me married. After marriage, I isolated myself. I preferred to be alone most of the time, cried myself to sleep daily, and never felt like seeing my parents or going back home for once.

During my loneliness, I felt a strong sense of warmth around me. Sometimes this feeling is compelling, comforting, and occasionally disturbing because it always makes me think of my tío.

On the other hand, my husband never questioned me. He always gave me my space and was very caring and understanding. Besides that, my in-laws treated me like their own hija. I never felt any defect in their love or their respect towards me.

Later, after a year of tío's (Uncle's) death, on a fine day of a new moon, I started taking a stand for myself. I promised myself that I would never feel this way again, and that's when my life took a turn. I started maintaining an organised life. I never depend on anyone, for that matter of fact.

Slowly, I began taking care of my husband's business. After learning my significant strategic way of dealing with business, my husband gave me all of his control. From then, I took control of his company, managed money, and brought notable changes in the family's lifestyle.

With the passage of days, things were going smoothly at my house. I had control over all the aspects. And no one ever belittled me, nor they disrespected me. My word is their act. I felt like a queen commanding everyone like I was making puppets play on a string. As time frittered away like this, I started becoming more authoritative. I set up rules and regulations. Because, why not? Everyone is dancing to my music. I started feeling like myself again; I enjoyed each second, minute, and day like this.

Everything was going great until one fine day; I received a call from my family talking about some bank taking possession of their house. What am I supposed to do about that? Like seriously, they come running to me now when they need help.

It was hilarious; it's just their karma hitting them back. Frankly speaking, I could have done something about the house, but I did not feel I wanted my hands dirty then. But, I never thought my papá (Father) would die for this reason.

When my papá (Father) discovered a bank taking possession, he felt a panic attack, and we lost him to a heart attack on the same day. Nevertheless, he is excellent; he lived 80 years of life. At that sharp end, I felt pity and had to take in all my family members and shelter them. Now that they are under my watch, I set up an obligation that applies to the entire coven in my house.

AARAV

Everyone was stunned when we encountered the disagreements between GG and Yamuna abuelita (Grandma). It was not like they never had any disputes; they had many, but this was more than a disagreement; it was an emotional wrath. Despite everything, I always wonder what made GG so strong for her age. Why is there a difference of opinion between GG and Yamuna abuelita (Grandma)? I have been stuck in this loop for a long time now. But now that Maneeksha has questioned GG, my curiosity built up to know GG's story.

I was keen to see every bit of GG´s history, not just me; even Sameeksha and Maneeksha were curious. We three sit there quietly, all our eyes glued to GG, who is now facing the window to start her tale.

GG lets out a deep exhale and begins to unfold our family history.

------_FLASHBACK_------

Back in 1907, farmers were forced to seek wage labour abroad due to the dismal living conditions in India during British rule. More than 6,000 Indian men immigrated to the United States via Canada in 1907.

The new community that sprang up due to interracial marriages were called "Mexican-Hindu," a broad term that wasn't entirely true as the term 'Hindu' referred to Hindustan rather than the religion. Approximately 80 per cent of these Indian men were Sikhs, and the remaining were Hindus and Muslims.

Despite the barriers of language and religion, all the Indian-Mexican couples found themselves to have much in common regarding cultural traits.

Food, for instance, was similar in both communities. Mexican cuisine, like Indian cuisine, was spicy and primarily relied on bread, vegetables, and meats that were typically boiled or fried. Mexican tortillas and Indian chapatis are nearly identical. The gorditas were stuffed with meat, while the paranthas were filled with vegetarian fare. Immigrants from Mexico and India grew up mostly in agrarian societies.

As a result, a shared thread of agriculture and farm life provided a stable foundation for the two groups to relate to one another.

The men often learned Spanish to communicate with their spouses. On the other hand, women learned how to cook Indian food, like making rotis and parathas, along with Mexican food, like Mexican rice.

The Luce-Celler Act of 1946 granted an annual quota for Indians who could migrate to the US. This Act changed the established Indian-Mexican family structure since men could now bring their Indian families and women to the United States.

Likewise, my husband Mahendra Varma's papá (Father) Vijendra Varma married a Mexican woman named Lisa Soler in 1935. And from then, Mexican culture was introduced into Varma's family, from food to all the Mexican festivals. Talking about festivals, the most celebrated festival among our family was "Día de los Muertos", which means "Day of the Dead". On 2nd November of every year, family and friends gather to pay respect and remember their family members who have died.

Día de los Muertos, or Day of the Dead, originated several thousand years ago with the Aztec, Toltec, and other Nahua people, who considered mourning the dead disrespectful. Death was a natural phase in life's long continuum for these pre-Hispanic cultures. The dead were still members of the community, kept alive in memory and spirit—and during Día de los Muertos, they temporarily returned to Earth.

The centrepiece of the celebration is an altar, or ofrenda, built in private homes. These aren't altars for worshipping; instead, they are to welcome spirits back to the realm of the living. As such, with offerings—water to quench the thirst after the long journey, food, family photos, and a candle for each dead relative. Marigolds are the main flowers used to decorate the altar. Some families place their dead loved one's favourite meal on the altar.

Along with Mexican culture and festivals, our family has also inherited a beautiful ancient codex laud key and Mexican lacquer box as a special gift.

This stunning ancient-looking, beautiful codex laud key and lacquer box are a fortune to any human being in this world as it is a medium to connect with their dead family on the Día de los Muertos festival.

Henceforth, we perform the Mexican ritual every year by decorating the house with marigold flowers and setting up an altar of pictures of our ancestors and the food they love the most. Afterwards, we place this beautiful ancient codex laud key inside the Mexican lacquer box to reunite with our lost loved ones.

'Wait.! Hold on!!' I say in disbelief, 'Is connecting with the dead people possible?'

'Not really,' says GG and continues, 'But with the codex laud key and lacquer box, our family can connect with our perished family members. Our family believes that if we do not keep our perished family in our memories, our perished family will gradually disappear from the "world of the dead". And subsequently, it is considered an essential ritual our entire family mandatorily follows.'

'Wow! That's unbelievable. I just can't imagine that there are things like this. Our family is a part of having super mystical powers,' says Maneeksha excitedly.

GG continues, 'This codex laud key and the ancient lacquer box are our traditional gift and a bridge to connect to our dead family.'

'We must cherish staying connected with our loved ones who have departed from this earthly realm, a gift beyond measure. Our gift is so precious no one in this world gets to do the thing which we do,' I say, almost proud.

'But what happened to this time-honoured tradition? Why are we no longer circling these sacred rituals?' questions Sameeksha.

With a downhearted expression and sadness filling GG´s eyes, she says, 'I know, right after we lost your great abuelo and our house to the bank, we also happened to lose the codex laud key.'

'Whatttt!' screamed all three of us, with utter shock.

'How can we lose the key when we know its importance, GG? What about the lacquer box? Is it still with us?' I question with a firm voice.

'We were all in haste to vacate the house as per the order; besides that, we were grieving over the loss of your great abuelo; in that hustle, we did fetch the lacquer box thinking the key was in the box,' said GG.

We three look at each other, not knowing what to say or how to react. There was silence for a while until Maneeksha jumped in with an idea.

'Idea! Why don't we go back to our old house and look for the laud key?' says Maneeksha.

'Hmmm, as soon as I discovered that the codex laud key was missing, I visited our old house, but...' GG stopped as tears filled her eyes.

'But? What happened, GG?' I question with curiosity.

'They have demolished our house,' says GG.

7

SAMEEKSHA

It was like a bombshell filling up the air. We have discovered so much history and shockers all at once that the three of us open our mouths.

'What!? Is our house demolished?!' I say with anxiety filling up my lungs.

'No, no, How could it be demolished?' says Maneeksha in an alarming voice.

'That's not the point. Now, How do we find the key then?' questions Aarav.

GG puffs out some air and says, 'I kept looking for the codex laud key everywhere possible but never got a hold of it.'

The three of us look at each other and walk towards GG; we pull her into a hug, assuring her that we will help her locate the laud key.

Aarav suddenly pulls out of the hug and asks, 'But GG, what is wrong with Yamuna abuelita (Grandma)? When she knows the importance of the rituals and the key, why does she not help you find the key?'

'Sí,' says Maneeksha adding to what Aarav said, 'Why does she not help you? Why are there so many disagreements between you guys?'

'I believe, It's just my fate. When your great abuelo was around, everything used to be structured, whether rituals or happiness amidst the family, but everything changed ever since he left us. My family was never the same; they never cared, loved, nor gave an ear to what I have to say since then. I think it is my age factor that is affecting our relations. But with age comes respect, here with age comes abandonment,' says GG with a trembling voice.

I could see her pain. I can feel what she is going through. Living in the same world, sharing the same family, and residing under the same roof should ideally foster a sense of unity and support.

However, my awareness that I hadn't fully recognised the extent of GG's pain and her challenges evoked profound regret. We three always spend quality time with her, but we couldn't be there for her in all these sufferings.

Reflecting on the times we spent together, the good memories shared, and the quality time enjoyed, I couldn't help but feel disappointed that I hadn't been there for her in her most difficult moments. It is a painful realisation that her struggles were carried alone, without the support and understanding she deserved.

The weight of GG's pain, which we now keenly felt, reminded me of the depth of her suffering. It became clear that her pain cannot be measured or compared, as everyone experiences and processes their emotions uniquely. Each individual's burdens and trials should be acknowledged and respected, regardless of how visible or invisible they may be.

We embrace her into our arms, the three of us almost crying.

Maneeksha says, 'GG, we weren't aware of this...,' I continue, 'We always thought you were a fantastic, trendy, fun-loving grandma who always enjoys being free-spirited. Still, we did not know what you were going through…'; Aarav continued, 'You know what, GG? You are very good at hiding pain, but why have you kept it from us?'

Now, everything started making sense to me; everything flashed right in front of my eyes as to why GG had a drinking problem, why she was independent, why everyone in the family gave no ear to her and why there was this cold treatment to GG from Yamuna abuelita (Grandma) all the time. I always thought it was just another mamá-hija (Mother-Daughter) disagreement, but it was more to it than just a disagreement.

As the puzzle pieces fell into place, I began to understand the underlying reasons behind GG's behaviours and the dynamics within our family. A deeper understanding emerged, shedding light on the complexities that had previously slipped away from my perception.

GG's drinking problem, which may have seemed isolated and puzzling, now took on a new context. It became evident that her struggles with alcohol may have been a coping mechanism, a way to numb the pain and mask the underlying emotional turmoil she experienced. This newfound insight allowed me to view her situation with compassion and empathy, recognising that her actions were not simply a result of personal choices but rooted in deeper emotional wounds.

The realisation that GG had been independent even at 82 took on a new significance. It became clear that her independence might have been borne out of a desire to assert control over her life and shield herself from further disappointment or hurt. Understanding this aspect of her character provided insight into her strength and resilience and the underlying vulnerabilities she may have concealed.

The strained relationship between GG and Yamuna Aublieta, which previously appeared as a series of disagreements, now revealed itself to be layered with unresolved issues and emotional distance. It became apparent that there were unspoken tensions and unresolved conflicts that had strained their connection over time. What might have seemed like a simple difference of opinion now carried the weight of deeper emotions and unaddressed wounds.

The realisation that there was more to GG's story than initially perceived allowed me to see beyond the surface-level interactions and understand the complex dynamics that influenced the family dynamics. It opened my eyes to the need for greater empathy, compassion, and active listening within the family, recognising that everyone has their struggles and pain, even if they are not readily apparent.

Maneeksha puffs out a range of anger filling within her; with a determined face, she turns towards us and says with a firm tone, 'No matter what, we will find the key not just for GG but also for our ancestors who have been long waiting for the sacred rituals.'

Aarav, GG and I look at her. And at that very instant, I felt a never-so-lively vibe. I can see the courage and the healthy mind aiming not just for the goodness of GG but also to shield our precious immortal ancestral connection.

Maneeksha hugs GG again and gives her reassurance. That's when Aarav and Maneeksha make a little gesture of nodding their heads and disperse to gather a whiteboard and marker. While Aarav sets the whiteboard, GG and I take our seats near the whiteboard.

'So, here's what we could do right now,' says Maneeksha, drawing a line on the centre of the whiteboard like a partition and writing "known" on the right-hand side of the board and "unknown" on the left-hand side.

'We all know we need a key, and the unknown part is, we do not know where we can find it,' continues Maneeksha, writing down the same.

'Mannu, to begin with, let's just go with the places where we can look for the key,' I say.

'Hmm, umm, in that case, I think that we should first start interrogating the people around our old house because there might be a higher possibility that the workers, whoever might have found the key, would have taken it to the owner and the owner might have handed it over to a nearby neighbour, informing them to hand it over to us,' says Aarav in deep thought.

'But what if that owner did not hand it over to any neighbour and kept the key to himself considering the antiqueness the key withholds,' says Maneeksha in a questioning tone.

'Well, in that case, I wonder if one of the workers might have picked it up, thinking that the ancient-looking key might fetch them money as it is antique. What do you think, GG?' I say and ask GG her opinion.

'You're right. Then, I believe we will have to start searching the details on who has taken the contract to demolish the house,' says GG.

We all nod our heads in agreement. 'But GG, how do we collect the company's details of who took the contract?' I question.

'Don't worry, I have my sources,' says GG, winking at me and smiling.

We all look at each other, and our smiles widen when Maneeksha turns to the board and writes "MISSION IMPOSSIBLE."

'Seriously, Mannu! You have to stop watching all those spy movies,' says Aarav, trying to control his laughter.

'Come on, bro, you should be lucky that I am a hardcore fan of detective movies and novels,' says Maneeksha, shrugging.

'Why is that so?' questions Aarav, trying to pull her leg.

'Little secret, I know the mindset of a detective, and of course, nevertheless, I act like one, so from now on, I will lead our MISSION IMPOSSIBLE and find the key,' says Maneeksha with pride in her voice.

We all laugh at once while GG says, 'Sí, our little detective, will lead MISSION IMPOSSIBLE.'

Mannu frowns as we laugh, but her face brightens as soon as GG lets her be the head for this MISSION IMPOSSIBLE.

I wink at Aarav and throw a pillow at him; he immediately gets in the play and throws the pillow on Mannu's face. Just like that, they kept roaming around the room, throwing pillows at each other. A little laughter ignites the room; I see GG laughing while Aarav and Mannu continue their play.

That smile, that laugh on GG's face, took me into a different world. Though she was happy with us at the moment, I could only think about the days she battled with her lonely self. At that very moment, I felt like I could do anything and everything for her by all means.

MANEEKSHA

Everyone in the house was fast asleep, but I, on the other hand, couldn't sleep after acquiring knowledge about my family.

I never really had a taste of what heartbreak could be. I always considered the following as heartbreaking: it's when one of your siblings has eaten your favourite ice cream, which you saved for later, or it's when you fought with your best friend because you haven't shared the silliest secret with them, Or it's when your dad has the remote while your favourite show is playing, and one of the most heartbreaking ones out of all is when your parents scold you because you hit your sibling, and at that very moment, you feel like leaving the house and going away somewhere. Like seriously, you start to get a feeling that your parents disowned you and they do not love you any more.

Besides all my reasoning of heartbreaking moments, today is when I realised what a real heartbreak would be like. It's tragic to know that your family is not by your side when you need them the most, it's frightening to fight a battle alone without any support, and mostly it is painful to let go of the ancient rituals that keep your dead family alive.

Discovering that your family is not there for you in times of need can be a shattering experience. The people supposed to provide love, support, and solace may be absent or distant, leaving you to navigate difficult situations alone. This sense of abandonment can leave you feeling vulnerable, scared, and emotionally isolated.

Fighting battles without support can be an unsettling task. It can feel overwhelming when you face hardships without the backing of loved ones. The world's weight rests solely on your shoulders, and the absence of a support system intensifies the pain and loneliness of the journey.

Additionally, letting go of ancient rituals that kept the memory of your deceased family members alive can be incredibly painful. These rituals often hold deep emotional significance, serving as a way to connect with and honour the past. Releasing them may feel like losing a tangible link to your heritage and the memories of your loved ones, further amplifying the heartbreak you experience.

I have seen people mourn the loss of their family, and their grief can never be expressed in words; with all this in place, it is a gift to stay connected with the dead family. Who has such a recourse to lead a life alongside their dead family?

Listening to our family history has not just blown my mind, but it has also made me believe in a mystical life. Though the story is heart-rending, being part of a family with a phenomenal secret is also lively.

My mind keeps wandering in all these thoughts as I switch television channels on mute.

Suddenly my heart skipped a beat, and I jumped from the sofa because of a sudden knock on my head. I let out a faint shriek while a hand from behind covered my mouth.

'Shh... Shhh! Keep quiet. It's me, Mannu.' says Sameeksha in a low tone.

'Usshh, you scared me, Sam,' I say as I take a few deep breaths while Sameeksha pats me to calm me down.

'Anyways, what are you doing here in the living room while everyone is asleep?' questions Sameeksha, sitting beside me.

'Don't you see, I was watching TV peacefully until you showed up out of nowhere and scared me?' I say, almost fussing.

'Really? In peace? If anyone walks in on you watching TV at this hour, then you will rest in peace forever. Look at the time; it's almost nearing 2:00 a.m.,' says Sameeksha, taking the television remote from my hands.

'Hmm, I know, Sam. But the thing is…' I say as I think about GG. But I stopped without speaking because I did not want to disturb Sameeksha after all we learnt today.

'Come on, spit it out, Mannu,' says Sameeksha, switching the TV channels.

I stay quiet for a bit when Sameeksha continues, 'Hmm; I get it, Mannu, even I cannot sleep after all these learnings and the most challenging thing to digest is knowing that GG has gone through a lot.'

'I want to end everything as quickly as possible; I can't see GG like this anymore after knowing about our family,' I say with my head down.

Sameeksha lifts my head, holds my face and looks into my eyes. 'Look at me, Mannu. I know it's difficult for us to see GG with a heavy heart but guess what? Everything is going to go back to how it was in the past. And this will happen very soon, do you know how?' says Sameeksha with a little smile.

'Soon…?! Really?' My eyes lit up. 'How?' I question Sameeksha with curiosity in my eyes.

'Because my twin hermana (Sister) is a detective, and she is the head of MISSION IMPOSSIBLE and will make sure to backtrack to how things were. And we all will work as a team to make sure to see a smile on GG's face. I promise,' says Sameeksha looking into my eyes with a smile.

I felt thrilled listening to that. I know for sure we are going to make it happen, not just for GG but also for our family.

I hug Sameeksha, and she takes me into her arms. We both close our eyes, staying in that hug while Sameeksha rocks me back and forth. As we both enjoy this time, I hear some faint sound from behind.

I pull out from that hug and say, 'Sam do you hear that?' I say with a bit of tension.

'Hear what?' questions Sameeksha.

'I think someone woke up and is heading to the living room,' I say, quickly grabbing the remote from her hands to turn the TV off.

'Mannu, it's no one. I don't hear any sound. Give me back the remote,' says Sameeksha and pulls the remote from my hand.

'No, Sam, you don't understand. Someone is up. Give me the remote quickly. Let's turn off the TV,' I say and snatch the remote.

As I snatch the remote, I accidentally turn up the volume high. At that moment, my future just flashed in front of my eyes. I see Yamuna abuelita (Grandma) walking towards us with a range of anger, shouting, 'How dare you try to watch TV at this hour! Get out of my house at this very instant,'

While I was having this flash of a nightmare, Sameeksha quickly grabbed the TV remote, and the power went out in seconds.

'Ussh, Gracias a Dios for saving us,' I say with a sigh of relief.

'Mannu, stay wherever you are. I am right here. I will get a candle,' says Sameeskha, almost whispering.

'No, stay with me. I am afraid of the darkness. Or else, I will also come along with you,' I say with fright.

'Hahahaa, the detective is scared of the darkness,' says Sameeksha sarcastically. 'Okay, come on then, hold my hand. We'll go together and fetch a candle. I am nearing you,' says Sameeksha.

'Sam, I am already holding your hand,' I say while I grab the fingers beside me and hold them tight.

'Come on, Mannu, not the time to play around. Okay, fine, I am sorry. I agree that you are as brilliant as a detective,' says Sameeksha, moving forward and stretching her hands, trying to find Maneeksha in this darkness.

'Lol, I know I am as brilliant as a detective. Now, if you walk quickly, we shall light a candle. This darkness is terrifying,' I say as I pull the hand and lock it in my arms.

'Mannu, I am not sure what you are holding onto, but let me tell you, I am not near you,' says Sameeksha.

I froze right then and there as soon as I heard Sameeksha. My arm is still locked with the not-Sameeksha 's arm. I try to feel the hand and fingers which I am holding, and that's when my brain does wonders. Within a fraction of a second, my mind declared it a ghost.

At that very moment, my soul left my body. I yelled as loudly as possible from the bottom of my lungs. My feet refused to move even a bit, but my mind ran as fast as it could. My inner voice kept telling me that it must be the spirits of one of our ancestors, it might have come to check on us as we got to know about them earlier today, or maybe it must have come to check on me in particular as I was the lead of MISSION IMPOSSIBLE.

I hear a chorus along with my screaming. It was Sameeksha who was yelling along with me. As I count the seconds nearing my death, a flash of light suddenly crosses my face.

9

AARAV

These faint voices in my ears keep me distracted while I think of a plan to find the codex laud key. I check where these voices are coming from. It's the living room; the voices are from the living room. I quickly reach out to my study table to grab a torch stick. I turn the torch stick on, but it looks dead. I smack the stick on my left arm for 30 seconds until I see its sparkle. I walk towards the door and go to the living room.

'Wait, hold on! What if there's a thief in the house?' 'You need to turn off the torch stick immediately,' echoes my mind. So, I quickly turn off the torch stick and take little tiny steps, ensuring not to alert whosoever is in the living room.

As I set foot in the living room, that's precisely when I heard Maneeksha scream, followed by Sameeksha. I quickly turn on the torch stick and flash it across the room. I spotted Maneeksha, Sameeksha and their little hermano Dhruv in that flash of light.

And suddenly, the electricity decides to return at that very moment. A loud TV volume, right next to it is "the trio". I get a clear view now. It's Maneeksha holding on to Dhruv, wearing all-black clothes and a Batman mask. Parallel to Maneeksha and Dhruv is Sameeksha. All three looked at me like they were caught in a bank robbery.

'Turn off the TV; you'll wake everyone up,' I tell them, almost tense.

As they return to their senses, Maneeksha and Sameeksha try to find the TV remote. Sameeksha turns off the television. The three of them look at each other in disbelief.

'What the hell, Dhruv!! You scared the shit out of me,' says Maneeksha, trying to breathe.

'WHAT IS HAPPENING HERE?' I hear a voice behind me.

All of us were in utter shock; our jaws dropped to our knees. It was Yamunna abuelita (Grandma). All the four of us look at each other, standing there still.

'Come on, open your mouths and speak,' yells Yamuna abuelita (Grandma).

'I… I.. uh… I heard a few noises and came to check,' I say, almost stammering.

Yamuna abuelita (Grandma) looks at the three of them for an explanation.

"We came to drink water," says Sameeksha and Maneeksha in unison.

'Both of you woke up in the middle of the night and came to drink water together in the living room, right?' questions Yamuna abuelita (Grandma) sceptically.

'Sí, uh.. I was thirsty and scared to leave my room at this late hour, so I woke Sameeksha up to tag along with me,' says Maneeksha.

'Yeah…. But… as soon as we heard a noise, we checked the living room and found Dhruv like this,' continues Sameeksha pointing at Dhruv.

That's when Yamuna abuelita's (Grandma's) focus shifted towards Dhruv, who was now cooking something in his mind to come up with a justification not only for his presence during this late hour but also for his attire.

Sameeksha and Maneeksha slowly slide off and stand beside me, trying to hide their mischievous smiles, while Yamuna abuelita (Grandma) looks at Dhruv from top to bottom.

'Why would you dress up like this and wear a funny-looking mask at this hour? What were you trying to do?' questions Yamuna abuelita (Grandma) seriously.

But Yamuna Abuelita's (Grandma's) sharp looks revealed she was not buying whatever came out of his mouth. Dhruv understood that very well and continued to say, 'This..' he looked at his dress and took out the mask, '... It is just my night dress, and this mask… is like a sleep mask. I wear it before I sleep so that light won't fall into my eyes and disturb my sleep,' he says with an awkward laugh looking at the mask. That's when I noticed instant regret on his face.

Sameeksha, Maneeksha and I very well knew he was up to something. We three were enjoying his little drama and trying to control our laughs with the justification he came up with. Besides that, his reasoning was insane, like, seriously, what kind of sleeping mask has holes for eyes? A sleeping mask is meant to cover your eyes. How did he even try to come up with that as a reason? Who does he think he was trying to fool?

Yamuna Abuelita (Grandma) did not speak a word. She turned back and started to walk towards the stairs. She stops before climbing the stairs and says, 'Dhruv, you better come up with a reasonable explanation tomorrow, or you will suffer for a week,' She then turns back, looks at us and says, 'Go to bed, all of you,' After which, she starts climbing the stairs and heads back to her room.

Once we got confirmation that she was back in her room. Sameeksha, Maneeksha and I ran to Dhruv.

'So, would you care to explain?' says Maneeksha, folding her arms.

'Why should I? If I knew you guys would turn in on me, I might have revealed that you two were watching TV at this hour,' says Dhruv with regret.

'Lol, look who is speaking. You always turn in on us most of the time. Anyways, you could have told Yamuna Abulieta we were watching TV, but how do you plan to explain your costumes,' says Sameeksha laughing sarcastically.

'Okay, fine, I am sorry I keep complaining about you guys, and I think we are even now,' says Dhruv.

'But Dhruv, what were you planning to do in those costumes?' I ask out of curiosity.

'Sí, what were you trying to do, and why haven't you spoken a word when you knew I was holding your hands while the power was out?' questions Maneeksha.

'Maybe, I guess, he did not want us to find out about him, or whatsoever he did. Is that right, Dhruv?' questions Sameeksha.

'No... I... I .. uh... was scared,' says Dhruv, almost hesitating to reveal the truth.

'Good! You should be sacred of your hermanas (Sister),' says Maneeksha with a broad smile as if she made an achievement.

But I could sense something was off. Dhruv's expression changed in the very instance as if he was alarmed.

'Scared of what?' I questioned.

When I asked him, he looked into my eyes seriously and said, 'I saw something. Something terrifying,'

Dhruv grabs the three of us by hand and makes us sit on the sofa. Sameeksha, Maneeksha and I looked at each other; that's when we understood there was something serious by the look on Dhruv's face.

'What is it, Dhruv? You are scaring us. What did you see?' says Sameeksha with fright in her voice.

'It's… it's about Yamuna abuelita (Grandma).' says Dhruv with wide eyes.

DHRUV

'It's a new moon day. I cannot set my foot out,' I told my friend Yash over a video call.

'So what? Why can't you?' questions Yash.

'You don´t understand, Yash. I will be a lump of dead meat if Yamuna abuelita (Grandma) finds out I set my foot out on a new moon day,' I say, trying to explain the consequences of my actions.

'Come on, man, don't be a coward. I know how much you were waiting for this day; now that we got a chance to sneak into my dad's secret library, you can´t back out at this last moment,' says Yash, almost disappointed.

'Let it be; we can sneak out next time, and mind that I may be a fun spoiler but not a coward. I just respect and follow our house rules,' I say, with instant anger piling up in my throat.

'Lol, that's what you are, just a wimp. If you aren't a wimp, prove that you can sneak out of your house and go to any extent for something you love,' says Yash as he lets out a sarcastic laugh.

'Don't play it cool when you are not. I am not falling for that. I don't have to prove anything to you. I would rather dare to find Yamuna Abuelita's (Grandma's) secret than sneak into your dad's secret library,' I say, spitting the anger out on Yash.

'Dhruv... It's not that, bro. I know it must be hard on you to follow such unreasonable rules. I am just concerned about you. Because of these stupid rules, you miss out on everything you desire. You have to do something about it apart from following it mindlessly,' says Yash with a worried expression.

I remain quiet. Taking my silence as a cue, Yash then continues.

'If you at least knew the purpose, you would be satisfied knowing that you are giving up on your interests for a valid reason. But, without knowing the reason, I think it is foolish. And for how long will you compromise like this?'

He has a point. 'Hmmm, you are right. I admire the beauty of antiques. I have waited for days to sneak into your dad's secret library to view the antique collections, and now when I finally have a chance, I am all tied up,' I say with disbelief.

'You see, this is what I was worried about. I did not want you to have any regrets,' says Yash.

I nod in agreement.

'Dhruv, don't get upset. My dad is considering revealing his secret library to the public before the exhibit community takes over. So, he is planning to host a TV show tomorrow, and I promise I will take you along with me before the TV show is hosted,' says Yash with excitement.

Listening to that, my face automatically gleamed, and with a broad smile, I said, 'Oh wow, that's terrific news.'

'Before that, let us focus on finding the reasons for these weird obligations. What do you say?' questions Yash.

'You are right. I don't want to be that person with regrets in life. I will start finding out the reasons. How about I start today by discovering the secrets of the new moon day?' I say with curiosity filling up.

'Very well. That is what I love about you, Dhruv. Go for it,' says Yash with a wink.

'Okay then, I will call you if I need anything. I think I will start by preparing a plan,' I say with a little smile.

'Sure thing. I am just a call away. Bye.' says Yash and disconnects the call.

For some reason, there is this unknown relief which I can feel. There is a weight lifted off my shoulders. Without delay, I quickly think of how to implement my strategies to spill the beans from Yamuna Abuelita (Grandma).

While I sat on the chair and tried to pen my strategy down, I somehow slid into the thoughts of my role in this family. Everyone in the family pampers me because I am the younger one. But, besides the pampering, no one has ever considered my opinions, thoughts, or interests; because of this, I have had this loneliness in my life for a long time now. Someone only bothers about me when I complain about my three siblings.

Aarav, Sameeksha, and Maneeksha never said anything to me, even after I bit their backs. I enjoy the unconditional love they shower upon me secretly. I know they love me so much, not just because I am their younger hermano but also because of my intelligence. They treat me well, understand my reasons or emotions, and, most importantly, keep me on my toes.

I love how they enjoy their time with GG. I always wish to be a part of their group, which is one reason I plan to slander their thoughts. I love how they consider thinking about my thoughts before doing anything.

One fine day, when I become an antiquary, I will make sure that my family regrets that they were not a part of my success. My love for antiques started when my school took me to a museum. That particular museum contained all kinds of ancient paintings, sculptures, and other important works of art. I loved reading about the history, culture, civilization, religion, art, and architecture through the antiques.

That was the day when I found the purpose of my existence. I performed research on many such museums around India. I happened to create a checklist of the museums I wanted to visit across India, starting with— National Museum Delhi, Indian Museum Kolkata, Government Museum Chennai, Chhatrapati Shivaji Vastu Museum Mumbai, Shankar's, International Dolls Museum Delhi, Salar Jung Museum Hyderabad, National Rail Museum Delhi, Calico Museum Ahmedabad, Dr Bhau Daji Lad Museum Mumbai, Napier Museum Trivandrum.

I don't know when I will check out my list, but there is one thing I know for sure: If I tie knots to these rules and restrictions, I will never be happy, nor will I fulfil my dreams.

And talking about which, I really must thank my best buddy Yash. He is thoughtful of all my likes and dislikes and knows how stuck I am to these obligations. Besides that, who would even think of sneaking someone into their papá's (Father's) secret library? Yash is very wealthy and always has rich friends accompanying him; despite that, he always tags around me, encourages me, and does anything just for my happiness. I am glad I have a friend like Yash, who motivates me to fulfil my dreams. I just want to show my thankfulness by finding the answers to this unreasonable set of rules. And I can achieve this only by revealing Yamuna Abuelita's (Grandma's) secret. Why does she have these weirdest rules? Why must we stick to these obligations? And most importantly, what is this new moon day all about?

Now is the perfect time to discover what this new moon day withholds. All these thoughts keep wobbling in my mind while I think of a plan, but nothing hits my brain. So I decided to stroll on the terrace in the fresh air to fetch some ideas.

As I set my foot out and headed for the stairs which led to the terrace, I noticed Yamuna Abuelita walking out of her room. I went to her to buy some information from her.

'Abuelita (Grandma), guess what?' I say to grab her attention. She stops and waits for me.

'I was thinking; we have never had any gathering or family time in so many years. We only gather for meals, but why don't we organise a fun family event?' I say, almost excited, blocking her way.

'Dhruv, we will never have any fun gatherings or events. Now, if you move out of my way, I must hurry somewhere; I am getting late,' says Yamuna Abuelita (Grandma) with a serious look.

I look at my wristwatch and say, 'It's 8:00 pm. Are you not coming for dinner then?' I asked her to know her plan for the night of the new moon.

I know she typically has no food on the new moon day and hides in the locked room where no one dares to set foot.

'Dhruv!! What is up with you? How dare you question me?! Don't you know, I skip my meals on a new moon day?!! Do I have to give you an explanation for everything now?' She yells at me and calls out to my mum, 'Meenakshi... Meenakshi... come here at this very instance!'

My mum comes running upstairs. 'What's the matter, Suegra (Daughter-in-law)?' questions my mum.

'Teach your hijo (Son) some manners. He is getting on my nerves,' says Yamuna Abuelita (Grandma) and hastily walks towards the locked room.

'Dhruv, what did you do? What made her angry?' questioned my mum, worried about me.

'I don't understand what made her angry. I usually find Yamuna Abuelita (Grandma) very unreasonable,' I tell my mum.

'Shh, lower your tone,' says my mum, looking left and right, not to be overheard by anyone. She continues talking almost in whispers.

'We all know how she is. We should never question her; we should only follow,' she says, holding my face and combing my hair with her fingers.

'If you need anything, ask me. Ask your mamá (Mother). I am right here,' she says as she kisses my forehead.

'Okay, mum, gracias.' I said and smiled at her.

'Come on now, help me set up the table for dinner. It's almost time,' she says, grabbing my hands as we walk to the dining hall.

After dinner at 9:30 p.m., I complete my dinner as quickly as possible and go to the terrace to think of an idea.

As I walk and take rounds on the square-shaped terrace, I smell a fragrance coming from the left-hand side of the terrace, which is towards the north direction. I follow the scent and halt to lean on the fencing wall. I look down to the ground floor to track the whereabouts of the scent. As I peeked, I noticed a tiny cloud of fumes and visible smoke coming out from a window. In that very instance, it was so evident to me that this window was of the locked-up room on the second floor of the building.

I started my estimations on how to reach the window to see what was happening in that room. I walk to the other three sides to check alternative ways or possibilities to reach the window. My mind starts running as fast as possible and finds two ways to reach the window.

One of the ways is to tie a rope around my waist and glide down until I get to the window, and the other way is from my room. As my room's window is just two windows away from the locked-up room, I can hold on to the head casing, side jambs, or sill of a window to move from window to window until I reach the window of the locked-up room.

The second idea seemed risky, so I considered pursuing the first option. Now that I know the plan, I head out to my room. I don't want to leave traces or gain any suspicion, so I thought I wanted it to be like a robbery. If at all anyone is awake or I get caught, I want to look like a thief who came for theft. I found my all-black jumpsuit in my wardrobe, which is perfect for my theme.

'Now, I need my face to be covered,' I say as I look for a face mask. 'Perfecto! I guess this will do,' I say as I pull out my Batman mask.

And now, we just have to wait for everyone to sleep. I wanted to wait until 12:30 a.m. before I started my set-up for the task.

At 12:27 a.m., I couldn't stop thinking about my plan or how to execute it. I have never been this curious to find out about something. As the time nears to accomplish my task, I become more restless. So, I dressed in black costumes and wore the Batman mask.

As soon as it ticked 12:30 a.m., I started to head to the terrace, thinking of making arrangements for the rope. I felt so disappointed as soon as I saw the terrace door locked.

'Ay! What the hell!!?? Why is this door locked?!!' I say as I feel disappointed. I never knew that they would lock even the terrace door. I quickly go downstairs to check where I can find the terrace keys.

As I climb the stairs, something clicks in my mind, 'Sí, I know where to find the keys,' I say to myself and head towards the diary in the living room, the "Book of Rules."

As I was at the living room entrance, I began to crawl to be on the safer side. I keep crawling until I reach the "Book of Rules." There is a large tray containing all the keys.

I slowly grab the keys without making any noise; I move my hands in search of the terrace key. 'No hurry, take your time,' I say to myself, 'There you are,' I smile as I find the keys.

I start to crawl again until I reach the stairs and take tiny steps as I climb the stairs. This robbery feels like an adventure, me wearing these costumes with a mask, crawling to collect the key, trying to break into the locked terrace, and finally finding the secret of Yamuna Abuelita (Grandma).

As I opened the lock, I headed south to collect a rope near the water tank. I quickly grab the rope and walk north towards my destination. I let out the rope towards the window to check its length.

'I am lucky; this rope is longer than I needed,' I say, and I see the time, 'It's nearing almost 1:00 am,' I say as I tie one end of the rope around my waist and the other end to the ladder in the south, maybe 50 meters away from the water tank.

I take a deep breath and step up on the terrace wall. I lower myself by gripping the rope tightly, trying to be as steady as possible.

In a matter of 20 mins, I was there, facing the window. As I reached the window, I tried gripping the window side jambs, which got me closer, more expansive, and had a better view.

A fog of smoke and fragrance fills the room. And in this misty smoke, I can see a shadowy figure. It's Yamuna Abuelita (Grandma), facing towards something, nodding her head, holding a bunch of "veritas de incienso" (Dhoop batti) in her hands.

As I tried to move forward, my hands lost a grip on the rope, making me slip. Right then, my body was pushed backward by a light breeze. I tighten my grip on the side jambs in haste, producing some faint noise. As I made the noise, I was terrified Yamuna Abuelita (Grandma) would catch me, but surprisingly there was no movement in Yamuna Abuelita (Grandma). She stood still in the same position, nodding as if she were having a conversation or an agreement.

I was baffled about what was happening; no other person was in that room. Who could she possibly be talking to? I looked around the room briefly; it was more like a storeroom. There were a few things in the room, a mirror, a single cot bed, something similar to a stand, two dim lights which gave a proper view of the surroundings, a few paintings, and a few covered photo frames hung on the walls. I wonder who could be in those photo frames.

While I observe everything in the room, I notice Yamuna Abuelita (Grandma) moving towards her right to set the "veritas de incienso" (dhoop batti) in a stand. As she moves, I see a medium-sized photo frame of a man, most probably a dead person, as the photo has a fresh garland around it, and I immediately try to recollect memories, but I couldn't possibly think who that would be.

I witness something terrifying as Yamuna Abuelita (Grandma) sets the "veritas de incienso" (dhoop batti) on the stand. 'THE PHOTO SPEAKS!' I say as I instantly get goosebumps. A shiver of cold sweat runs down my spine. The dead person in the photo speaks, and most shockingly, Yamuna Abuelita (Grandma) responds to what he speaks. Both of them are conversing… In the photo frame, Yamuna Abuelita (Grandma) talks with a deceased person.

After eye witnessing such an incident, I no longer tend to have that strength. My body was drenched in sweat. 'I have to leave from here at this very instant,' I say to myself as I loosen the grip on the side jambs and grab the rope tighter. I try to pull myself up, but the fright makes me weak and takes away my breath. I try to gulp down some air. 'I will surely die if I don't move fast,' I say to myself to push myself as much as possible.

I somehow managed to pull myself up. My legs are shaky, my fingers froze, and I am sweaty. I quickly pull up the rope and throw it near the tank as it was. I head out from the terrace, ensuring it's locked as it was, and quickly run down the stairs without making a noise. As soon as I reach the living room, I notice Sameeksha and Maneeksha watching TV on mute. I quickly bend down and crawl towards the kitchen to drink water and quench my fright.

I make sure to drink as much water as I can. I just want to go to my room and try to understand and sink into reality, but I remember having to place the terrace key from where I picked it.

I slowly kneel and crawl as I return from the kitchen to the living room. I can see Sameeksha and Maneeksh fighting for the remote, and that's when the power is out. I quickly reach the stand where the "Book of Rules" is placed to mix the terrace keys into the other cluster of keys. I take massive relief of breath and make use of the darkness. However, unfortunately, Maneeksha holds on to me, thinking I am Sameeksha.

YAMUNA

My tío (Uncle) loved me the most. He taught me how to walk, talk, eat and, most importantly, live as I like. No one dared to question me for 18 years because of tío (Uncle) by my side. He was my strength. He won't keep quiet if anyone tries to correct or discipline me. My mamá (Mother) and papá (Father) were happy with the bonding I had with tío (Uncle), but at the same time, they were also concerned that I would be spoiled with all the love he showered upon me.

Despite my authoritative nature, I enjoyed the influence I had from my tío (Uncle). With tío (Uncle) by my side, I can do whatever I want. I can make anyone dance to my music. I always enjoy being the captain of my ship, and on the other hand, I also love how tío is the engine that pumps up the energy my ship requires.

After tío (Uncle) left us, everything changed. My family never treated me the same, and I was never the captain of my ship. They put my opinions, thoughts aside and never cared about my feelings. Besides the fresh wounds of losing tío (Uncle), my heart shattered with this sudden change of treatment by my family.

In a blink of an eye, I was married. I was outraged, anguished, adrift, unhinged and felt uneasy. I did not know what to do. I had a pile of mixed emotions. Most of it was anger. I was angry with my family for getting me married, and besides that, I was angry with my tío for leaving me in this state. I was angry at every little thing that came my way. I did not know where or how to proclaim this anger at its peak. I reached a state of mind where I started hating myself. I did not know how to deal with myself. I was lost and was drowning in this sorrow.

One fine day, after almost 12 months, I finally confronted my tío (Uncle).

——--23rd April 1978- New moon day

'Yamuna, I know you miss your tío (Uncle),' says my husband, Raghuveer.

I remain quiet, looking outside the window.

'They say time heals everything, but it's not entirely correct. Time doesn't cure anything for you. During that time, you learn how to endure and deal with the pain… until you get used to it,' I say, looking outside the window in lost thoughts.

'I know it's hard on you, but this is life; you must move on. It's already been a year now. For how long will you be like this?' he questions me with a sympathetic look.

He holds me by my shoulders and turns me towards him; he then lifts my chin. 'Look at me, Yamuna,' says Raghuveer.

He holds my face and speaks, 'When do you think people die?' he questions me.

I remain silent, looking into his eyes. Taking my silence as a cue, he continues.

'People die only when they are forgotten. Like you remember your tío (Uncle), your tío (Uncle) still remembers everything about you. He probably desperately wants to talk to you,' he says.

My eyes welled up, and tears slowly slid down my cheeks.

'Tears are more precious than smiles, don't let these teary eyes dominate your beautiful smile. Time will gradually heal the pain in your heart,' says my husband as he kisses my forehead and wipes my tears away.

'Remember, I am always here for you. I love you,' he continues and pulls me into a hug.

I fall into his arms and stay there momentarily, 'Uh… I think I want to go for a drive…' I say. I pause for a bit and then continue, 'Alone. Can I?'

'You don't have to ask for anyone's permission. This is your kingdom, and you are the queen,' says Raghuveer with a smile and then continues, 'But… Promise me that you will keep yourself busy after today. I don't like to see you in lost thoughts like this anymore. The queen not only rules the kingdom but also looks after the business. I want you to be the chairman of our company; think about it,' says Raghuveer.

I nod in agreement while he hands me the car keys.

'Are you sure you will be okay alone?' questions Raghuveer with a slight concern.

'Don't worry. I will be okay. I just want to spend some time alone outside,' I say.

'Okay, careful,' says Raghuveer and turns back to leave the room.

I wait until my husband leaves the room. As he leaves the room, I walk up to the mirror just to get some assurance and confidence from myself.

I look into the mirror, wiping off my tears. I looked at my eyes. That's exactly when I knew where I had to be. I quickly walk out of my room and head towards the car.

As I start the car, the engine ignites, and I stomp the accelerator and zoom off to where I can confront my tío (Uncle). I know I cannot see my tío (Uncle) on the festival of "The Day of the Dead" because his body did not get the last rites, and I do not want to set foot in the house of the people who have belittled me, my thoughts and my opinion. I want to create my means of communication with the dead, but I do not know how.

A few thoughts keep me occupied as I drive the car. Usually, most of the Hindus tend to bury the body instead of cremating it. The Gita says: "Just as old clothes are cast off and new ones worn, the soul leaves the body after death and enters a new one."

Hindus believe that burning and destroying the body helps the departed soul overcome any residual attachment it may have developed for the deceased person.

However, although our family belongs to the Hindu community, we follow body burial instead of cremating, as we hold strong cultural roots in Mexican traditions. In our Mexican culture, a vigil is held with family and friends after death for 24-48 hours. They will eat and drink together, and guests will pray and bring the family gifts. The deceased will be buried with their clothing and essential possessions. This traditional burial is a more popular choice among Mexicans. Either way, families like to have a spot to return to on special days to remember their loved ones. Similarly, all dead ancestors are celebrated yearly on All Souls Day, the "Day of the Dead."

These traditional burials are more important, especially in our family, as we honour the dead by keeping their names and stories alive for all generations because of the gift that we withhold.

I slam the brakes to a halt as I reach my destination. It's the graveyard where my tío (Uncle) is buried. I get down and lock the car. I slowly start walking towards my tío's (Uncle's) gravestone. Suddenly, everything seems to slow down—the time, the air, the birds, the trees—as I walk. I can feel the pain sinking into my bones like a needle; my throat quivers as I shriek. I stand frozen on my feet, fall on my knees, and explode like a volcano. I flare out all my anger as I cry and scream out of my lungs.

After venting out my heart, letting out all the mixed feelings I bottled up, I return home and feel like writing a letter to tío (Uncle). I sit peacefully at the study table, looking at the plain sky with no sight of the moon. I puff out a sigh of breath and grab a pen and a piece of paper.

Dear Tío (Uncle),

Time passed quickly when you were with me. And now, time has stopped ticking since you left. My world is different without you. Realising you won't return is killing me. You promised to be with me forever; what happened to that promise? I hate you for making me so vulnerable. You are the only person I love the most and the only person I hate the most. I want to have at least one good conversation with you. I just want to see you one last time. I want to return in time to relive our moments and cherish your existence. Come back, tío (Uncle), come back for me. I miss you a lot.

With Love,

Yamuna.

A few tears roll down my cheeks as I finish the letter. I then fold it up in quarters and go to the storeroom to find his photo. I look at that wide smile and the sparkling eyes in the picture, and I want to smile back at him; instead, my lips automatically frown looking at him.

I glimpse him for a second and leave the letter at the edge of the photo frame. 'I wish you could read this letter to know how I feel,' I say to the photo and turn the other way.

Tiny little goosebumps start to bring a shiver down my spine because of a voice from behind, "Did you miss me?" said the voice.

I hear my tío's (Uncle's) voice like an enchantment filling the air. It feels surreal until I turn back to see the photo of tío (Uncle) talking to me. And from that moment, I am never the same again.

I have waited for the new moon every month since I knew I could talk to the person I love the most. A wave of emotions washed over me as I discovered my ability to communicate with my deceased tío (Uncle) through a photo on every new moon day. Initially, I felt a mixture of disbelief, astonishment, and curiosity, unsure if what I was experiencing was real or a figment of my imagination.

As I delved deeper into these interactions, my feelings evolved. Each new moon day brought me a sense of anticipation and longing as I eagerly awaited connecting with my beloved tío (Uncle). The moments leading up to our communication would be filled with excitement and nervousness, wondering what messages or guidance he would impart.

During our conversations, I experienced a range of emotions. A profound sense of comfort and solace would wash over me as I felt the presence of my tío, as if he were still by my side, providing guidance and support. This connection may have instilled a sense of reassurance, knowing that our bond exceeded physical limitations.

My heart, however, would also be touched by bittersweet sorrow. Realising that these interactions were limited to new moon days would weigh on me. The longing to have my tío (Uncle) physically present, to share in life's joys and challenges, could stir up feelings of hope, yearning, and even a tinge of sadness.

Yet, amidst the mixed emotions, there was also profound gratitude. I cherish each conversation, treasuring the opportunity to maintain a connection with my tío (Uncle), even in his absence. The knowledge that our bond persisted beyond the realms of the physical world would give me strength and a sense of continuity.

Ultimately, my feelings would be deeply personal and unique to me. The ability to communicate with my tío (Uncle) on every new moon day offered me a precious opportunity for continued connection, healing, and a sense of spiritual guidance in my life.

GG

_NEXT DAY_September 25th, 2022

'You won't believe this GG,' says Maneeksha with wide eyes.

'Sí GG, I saw it with my eyes,' adds Dhruv.

'Do you think something like that is possible or even real?' says Sameeksha, almost sceptical.

'You never know, Sam,' replies Aarav.

All four of them keep talking at once, surrounding me. I sit silently, trying to understand their expressions, body language, and tone. I came to recognise that they had witnessed a bolt from the blue.

'Okay. Okay.. vamos one by one. Shall we?' I say, clearing my throat.

'GG listen to us carefully,' says all four of them in unison as they take seats, forming a semi-circle around me.

'Dhruv saw Yamuna abuelita (Grandma) talking to a person in the photo,' says Maneeksha, almost whispering.

'Okay...?' I say, shrugging to know more details.

Aarav knocks on Maneeksha's head and says, 'The person in the photo also spoke to her,' says Aarav with wide eyes.

'Sí GG, I saw it with my eyes. It was a photo of a dead person. The photo frame had a garland around it. Yamuna abuelita (Grandma) was holding a bunch of veritas de incienso (incense sticks) and was talking to the photo. I was terrified when the photo replied, and I am still shaking thinking of what I saw,' continues Dhruv.

'Really? How is that even possible?' I say with utter shock.

'Exactly, even I feel the same, GG,' says Sameeksha.

'But GG, think of it this way, what if Yamuna abuelita (Grandma) already has possession over the key? She might be talking to the dead and hiding from everyone?' says Maneeksha.

'Hmm, that might not be the case. If she is using the key, she must use the lacquer box,' I say as I drift into thoughts and then continue, 'The key doesn't work without the lacquer box. Moreover, the box and the key only work on "The Day of the Dead" festival.'

'I see; then she must be using something else,' says Aarav.

'Wait…! What key? What box? Did I miss something?' Questions Dhruv, looking at everyone.

'I wonder who she was talking to?' says Sameeksha, ignoring Dhruv.

'Dhruv, by any chance, did you see his face? Do you recognise the person in the photo?' questions Maneeksha.

That was an excellent question. I turned towards Dhruv, waiting for his answer. I notice Aarav, Sameeksha, and Maneeksha looking at Dhruv for an answer.

Dhruv looks at all of us at once and says, 'Before I answer, can someone tell me about the key and the box?' questions Dhruv, folding his arms.

'Uff, come on, Dhruv,' says Aarav.

'Our family holds this ancient codex laud key and a lacquer box, allowing us to see our dead family on the festival day,' I say, looking at Dhruv.

'No way!' says Dhruv while his jaw drops. 'Is it possible? By the way, what do we do on this Day of the Dead festival?' questioned Dhruv curiously.

'Sí Dhruv, it's very much possible with the key and the box. But, we lost the key because we could not see our dead family and stopped the ritual of celebrating the Day of the Dead festival,' says Maneeksha.

'Moreover, The Day of the Dead festival is a Mexican festival which happens every year on the 2nd of November, where we celebrate the living of the dead. And on that day, we have this mystical power to see our dead family through the key and box,' continues Sameeksha.

'This is unbelievable. But, I believe it after witnessing the most surreal thing,' says Dhruv, nodding.

'Now, will you tell us about the person in the photo frame? Do you recognise that person?' questions Aarav.

'Hmm, let me think...' says Dhruv rolling his eyes up as if he is recalling and continues, 'Not really, I have never seen that person before,' says Dhruv, scratching his chin, 'But surely I haven't seen any kind of box or a key,'

All of us look at each other in disappointment.

'Idea!' shrieks Maneeskha and continues, 'GG, do we have any old photo albums? Maybe Dhruv can point out the person from our old family photo albums,'

'Mannu, how sure are you that the person in the photo belongs to our family?' questions Sameeksha.

'Sam has a point but what's wrong in ruling out our options?' says Aarav.

'Wait, let me gather all the photos that I have,' I say.

I quickly get up and make my way towards the storage racks. As I search for the photo albums near my filed documents, my eyes fall on an old brownish paper with eye-catching cursive handwriting. I take the old brownish paper to get a clear view.

Date: 2nd February 1955

The truth is so great that I wouldn't like to speak, sleep, listen, or love. To feel trapped, with no fear of blood, outside time and magic, within your fear, your great anguish, and the heart's beating. All this madness, if I asked it of you, I know, in your silence, there would be only confusion. I ask you for violence in the nonsense, and you give me grace, light, and warmth. I'd like to paint you, but there are no colours because there are so many, in my confusion, the tangible form of my great love.

It's a love letter from my husband before we got married. He loved me so much. And here I am, struggling to keep his dream alive. He only wanted to see everyone in the family happy and keep Varma's family members alive even after their deaths. I hug the letter as a few tears roll down my cheeks.

'What's wrong, GG?' says Sameeksha running towards me.

Aarav, Maneeksha, and Dhruv quickly look at me and come towards me. At the same time, Maneeksha says, 'Are you crying, GG?'

I open my eyes to see all four of them gathered around me. I nod as I say, 'No, nothing; this letter made me think of your great-grandpa.'

'Show us,' says Aarav, taking the letter from my hands.

Aarav reads it aloud for the rest of them, and I get instant reactions, 'Oh mi, it's a love letter,' says Dhruv.

'Aww, GG! Great-Grandpa is so sweet,' says Maneeksha.

'He loved you so much,' says Sameeksha.

'As a child, I have memories of being with you and playing with Sam and Mannu. I don't have any memory of my Great-Grandpa. I wish he were with us right now,' Aarav says, frowning.

'You are right, bro. Though we were just a few miles away, we never got to see our great grandpa or spend time with him because of Yamuna abuelita (Grandma)," says Maneeksha while Sameeksha continues, 'Sí, I wish he was with us.'

I can see the disappointment on all four faces, and I pull them into a hug.

'But did you guys not say that we still can talk to him if we had that key and the box,' says Dhruv pulling out from the hug.

'Sí, we first need to find the key to do that,' says Aarav.

'Oh yeah, we misplaced the key. That completely slipped my mind,' says Dhruv, rubbing the tiny back of his head.

'Come on now, let's not waste any more beats. It's time for MISSION IMPOSSIBLE,' says Maneeksha.

Everyone nods in agreement while Sameeksha grabs the photo album and hands it to GG.

'Come on, kids, let me show you our Family photo album,' I say, walking towards the bed.

I sit at the centre of the bed, and all four gather around me, forming a semi-circle. I open the photo album and fall into a pit of nostalgic black holes. With each photo, I give some background of the captured memory.

Dhruv suddenly stops as we skim through the photos. Dhruv suddenly stops and grabs the album from my hands.

'This is it! He was the person from the photo,' says Dhruv pointing out a man holding a child.

'Show me,' says Aarav, pulling from Dhruv's hands to look closer. 'I don't recognise him either,' says Aarav.

"Give it to me," says Sameeksha, pulling the album from Aarav. 'Wait, I think I recognise this little girl,' says Sameeksha.

'Let me see,' says Maneeksha as she takes hold of the album. 'Is she Yamuna abuelita (Grandma)?' questions Maneeksha, showing it to me.

I take the photo album and take a closer look. It is the photo of Narendra Varma holding my baby girl, Yamuna.

SAMEEKSHA

'This is your great grandpa's hermano (Brother), Narendra Varma,' says GG as she puffs out some breath and then continues, 'The girl he is holding is Yamuna. She had a great bonding with her tío. As a little girl, the only time Yamuna was genuinely happy was when we had him around us. We lost him in a car accident,' says GG.

'What happened after that? How did Yamuna abuelita (Grandma) overcome this hardship?' questions Aarav.

'She was precisely 18 years old when we lost Narendra Varma. It was tough on everyone, especially her. We were concerned about her a lot, but we also had a significant responsibility of getting her married that year,' GG says with a sigh.

'What? Why so? Why in that year? When was she going through so much .' I ask, almost in shock.

'Well, it was considered auspicious to conduct the marriage of a close family member within a year of the death of a person in the family,' says GG.

'So, what happened after her marriage? How did she cope with all these?' questions Maneeksha.

'Hmm, Yamuna was very naughty yet authoritative since childhood. When Narendra Varma was around, he did not let anyone question Yamuna. She was very pampered by him; they both spent most of their time together. It felt very nice to see their bonding. But since Narendra Varma left us, Yamuna was never the same again; she never spoke a word. She was lost in her thoughts and used to grieve.' GG says and looks down with tears rolling in her eyes.

GG slides away the now falling tears with her palm and continues, 'After... After she got married, she never returned to our house. She started avoiding us, and we never forced her because we understood her anger, but we always believed she would understand our reasons and come back to us, but...' GG breaks down into tears.

The four of us look at her and give her a few seconds. Maneeksha and I rub her back while she cries.

GG brushes off her tears with force this time and goes on, 'But most shockingly, she never stepped into our house after she got married.' GG's eyebrows frown, 'Besides that, while she knew about the bank taking over our home, she did nothing. She could have helped us save the house with all her power. If she had done that, we would still have your great-grandpa and the ongoing rituals with us, but she failed. She failed not just us, our entire family, our ancestors, and most importantly, she failed herself.' says GG, puffing out some breath.

Dhruv quickly grabs a water bottle from the side stand and gives it to GG, 'GG. I may be too young to say this to you, but hear me out—When everything goes to hell, your family stands by you without flinching. And remember, we are family, though Yamuna abuelita (Grandma) failed us right now, at some particular point, be it soon or after ages, she will realise one day and stand up for us,' says Dhruv.

Aarav, Maneeksha, and I look at each other, almost very proud of our little hermano. Though naughty and keeps pulling our legs, he is very thoughtful.

After listening to Dhruv, GG quickly hugs him and says, 'Sí..! You are right. We are family; we should stand by each other no matter what,' says GG.

The three of us join their hug as I say, 'Yamuna abuelita (Grandma) will realise it very soon,'

'Sí, she will realise very soon,' says Aarav, Maneeksha, and Dhruv in unison.

We stay in that hug for some time when Maneeksha pulls out from the hug and says, 'Okay, now that we got a few leads, where do we start?'

'That's right; we have few leads now. We know Yamuna abuelita (Grandma) is talking to her tío (Uncle) without the source of the key and the box. We need to find out how she is doing that. And also, we need to track the key as quickly as possible.' says Aarav.

'Let's do one thing; we shall split up in teams then and start our hunt from today itself,' I say excitedly.

'Yeah, great idea Sam. I was thinking the same thing,' says Mannu winking at me.

'Uh… ah… I.. I.. don't think I can join you today,' says Dhruv hesitantly.

'What happened to that? "We are a family and should stand up for one another" quote,' says Maneeksha mocking Dhruv.

Mannu's mocking-filled humour was in the air, and Aarav, GG, and I tried to control our laughter.

'Come on, Mannu, that's not a quote; it was from the bottom of my heart. And also, I already have plans with my friend, which I missed yesterday because of Yamuna abuelita's (Grandma's) new moon day rule.' says Dhruv.

'Okay, I agree it's from the bottom of your heart. But if I may ask, what plans are more important than this?' questions Maneeksha.

'Sí, It is essential. I can't miss it even today. If I miss it now, I won't be able to see it again.' says Dhruv with much emphasis.

'What is it about Dhruv?' I ask with some curiosity after looking at his strong will.

'Sam, you know my friend Yash right? That guy's papá (Father) holds a secret library of antique things, so he considers revealing it to the public before handing it to the exhibit community. So, for that, he will be hosting a TV show today.' says Dhruv with lots of excitement, 'I am lucky to have a friend like Yash; before anyone else, I can sneak into his papá's (Father's) secret library,' says Dhruv.

'Oh wow, that's so nice.' says GG smiling at him, almost proud of him.

'Hey, Dhruv, that's wonderful. I know how fond you are of antiques, and you must be happy to be the first person to view the secret library then.' I say with a wide smile.

"So happy for you, Dhruv.' says Aarav with a wide smile.

'But Dhruv, since this is your first day joining our MISSION IMPOSSIBLE, I can give you an exception only for today.' says Mannu folding her arms.

Dhruv keeps looking at everyone with blank faces out of confusion, 'MISSION IMPOSSIBLE?' he says with a question on his face.

'Oh, that's the name given to our mission to find the key, and Mannu will be leading this MISSION IMPOSSIBLE.' I say, pointing at Maneeksha.

Dhruv lets out a sarcastic laugh, 'Lol, Manu, good job.' says Dhruv.

'You…!! go, get out of here.' says Maneeksha with the slightest of anger.

'Alright then, I will go now,' Dhruv keeps laughing continuously as he walks out of the room

'Wipe that bloody smirk out of your face Dhruv,' yells Maneeksha and continues 'Alright, now back to our mission. As Sam said, we shall split into teams. Aarav and GG will work together and reach out to the contractor today. At the same time, Sameeksha and I will try to gather more information about Yamuna Abuelita's source of communication with the photo.' says. Maneeksha.

'That sounds perfect.' says GG.

'Alright, let's disperse and not waste any more time,' I say.

Thud A loud noise from the living room distracts us. We all quickly ran towards the living room.

MANEESKHA

A medium-sized book standing next to the TV was on the floor, with all the books scattered; right next to it was Dhruv facing Yamuna abuelita (Grandma), whose eyes were boiling by now. Everyone gathered in the living room in shock. GG, Aarav, Sam, and I are watching the show from upstairs, tension filling the house.

On the other hand, Dhruv is carefree, as if nothing has happened. He was fantastic, folding his arms and looking at everyone, including Yamuna abuelita (Grandma).

'WHAT NONSENSE IS THIS DHRUV?' yells Yamuna abuelita (Grandma) with anger piling up her throat.

'Dang it! Now do I need to have an explanation for this too? Come on, Abuelita, don´t be silly,' answers Dhruv recklessly.

'What….! What the hell is he doing?!!' I mumble as GG, Aarav, Sameeksha, and I look at each other.

'We need to stop this,' says Aarav walking towards the stairs. Sam and I follow Aarav.

'MEENAKSHI! WHAT IS WRONG WITH YOUR HIJO (Son)?' shouts Yamuna abuelita (Grandma) with a range of anger, now painting her face red.

'Uh... Dhruv, what are you doing? Come here and apologise to Yamuna abuelita (Grandma).' says mamá (Mother).

'Why should I mamá (Mother)? She is the one who needs to apologise to everyone in this house.' says Dhruv.

We all lost our minds when he said that; everyone was in utter shock, their jaws dropping to their legs.

My legs were almost shivering while we rushed down the stairs to stop the little drama now turning huge.

'No, no, no, what is he doing? We should not have told this guy any of this.' I mumble to myself.

'HOW DARE YOUR HIJO (Son) QUESTIONS ME? HE IS SIMPLY GETTING ON MY NERVES. HE IS SPOILED WITH ALL THE PAMPERING YOU ARE DOING.' says Yamuna abuelita (Grandma), spitting out her anger on mamá (Mother).

'Dhruv, what has gotten into you? Apologise to your abuelita (Grandma) at this very instance,' says mamá (Mother) with anger yet concerned tone.

Sameeksha and I halt as Aarav stops, rolling his eyes; he must be thinking of a plan. 'What can we do? What can we do?' I keep mumbling to myself.

'What for? abuelita (Grandma) asks everyone for reasoning and explanation, but have we ever considered asking about what she does?' He says with a firm tone.

'He completely lost it,' I say, looking at Aarav and Sameeksha.

'Idea!' says Sameeksha.

'ENOUGH! YOU SPOKE A LOT. NO ONE QUESTIONS ME IN THIS HOUSE!! IN MY HOUSE! NOW TELL ME, WHAT WERE YOU DOING

YESTERDAY IN THOSE WEIRD COSTUMES AT A WEIRD HOUR?!!' questions Yamuna abuelita (Grandma).

'Dhruv, Dhruv, Dhruv…' says Aarav, distracting everyone and continuing with a nervous laugh, 'lol, what are you doing, Dhruv? This is not how you do it,' says Aarav, increasing his laughter volume.

'Hello, guys! So here is my little hermano (Brother),' I say, pointing out at Dhruv with my front camera on and talking into it as if I am recording a video.

Sameeksha jumps into the video and continues from where I left off, 'Who has failed to prank everyone in the house,' she quickly grabs the phone from my hands, captures everyone in the place, and stops near Yamuna abuelita (Grandma). 'So guys, this is not the way to prank anyone, but let's try to find out how the house feels about this,' says Sameeksha. At the same time, Aarav jumps into the video and continues, 'Let's start with our primary victim.' says Aarav grabbing the phone from Sameeksha's hands and questioning Yamuna abuelita (Grandma).

'ENOUGH OF THIS NONSENSE! STOP IT RIGHT AWAY,' Yells Yamuna abuelita (Grandma), shouting at the top of her lungs. Her screaming this time brought goosebumps to all of us, and we jumped in our places. The situation was heating up, so we immediately dropped this act.

'LINE UP! ALL THE FOUR OF YOU!' says Yamuna abuelita (Grandma).

All four of us lined up chronologically with our heads hanging downwards and our eyes fastened to the floor.

'DON'T MAKE FOOLS OUT OF YOURSELF. I NEED A PROPER EXPLANATION OF ALL THIS NONSENSE. ESPECIALLY FROM DHRUV,' says

Yamuna abuelita (Grandma) with a serious tone, glaring at Dhruv.

'Any which way she is going to punish us, then why need explanation,' whispers Dhruv into my ears.

'Shh, Dhruv, shut up your mouth.' I replied, almost afraid Yamuna abuelita (Grandma) would hear.

'WHAT ARE YOU MURMURING?' questions Yamuna abuelita (Grandma), looking at Dhruv.

'Abuelita,' says Sameeksha, trying to grab Yamuna abuelita's (Grandma's) attention towards her, 'actually, we have a youtube channel for which we came up with a prank video,'

'So, you! You guys wanted to make me a fool in front of everyone? The whole world?' questions Yamuna abuelita (Grandma).

'Abuelita, it's not like that,' interrupts Dhruv.

'Shut up, Dhruv,' says Aarav and continues, 'You made it worse. Apologise to Abuelita now,' he gestures to Aarav, rolling his eyes.

'Abuelita, we are sorry. We just wanted to be famous,' I say with crocodile tears, 'We just want to earn fame and make you proud.'

'We are sorry, Abuelita (Grandma).' the four of us say simultaneously.

'Your sorries won't work, all the four of you are grounded, and your phones are confiscated, mainly because of Dhruv's unreasonable behaviour, appearance and talking.' says Yamuna abuelita (Grandma) and walks upstairs.

She pauses briefly on the stairs and continues, 'All four of you will be returning to the room in the basement. You only come out during meal hours or if there is any requirement for household chores. Based on your behaviour, I will set you all free, until then, do not even think of playing around just like before. And, Finally, this kind of behaviour is not entertained in my house. Mind it!' she says and turns back in haste heading towards her room.

All the people who had gathered in the house slowly dispersed.

As soon as Yamuna abuelita (Grandma) leaves, Dhruv starts, 'What!! No way! I need to go to my friend's place! This is not fair!!' sulking.

'Then, who asked you to create a scene out of nowhere? You should have minded your business.' says Sameeksha.

'Sam….' says Dhruv with a crying face.

Dhruv looks at me with puppy eyes. I roll my eyes and shrug as if I can't help. He then turns to Aarav and says, 'Bro, only you can help me now.'

'No, not after all you did now.' says Aarav folding his arms.

'Come on, now, enough of your discussions. Did you not hear what Yamuna abuelita (Grandma) said? Head to the basement immediately,' says mamá (Mother) angrily.

'Mum…' says Dhruv, but mamá (Mother) gives a deaf ear to him and gestures for everyone to move. I can sense how angry she was with all of us.

Without speaking, we all head to the basement as mamá (Mother) follows us. As we reach the cellar, mamá (Mother) stops us in the hallway. The hallway has two rooms adjacent to each other. The room to the left is locked, while the room towards the right is unlocked. The four of us had never been to the basement before. Everything looked amusing to us because of the vintage look of the hallway.

As we wait and watch, mamá (Mother) unlocks the room towards the left and lets us all in. As soon as I enter the room, the first thing that hits me is the smell – disinfectant, bleach. A lot of both, as if to clean the grey surface of all stains and odours and erase the room's history.

'Wow, I have never been here,' says Dhruv admiring the room.

'Yeah, we too. We have never seen it or been here before.' says Aarav, speaking for Sameeksha and Me.

'Okay, now, all of you... Hand over your phones,' says mamá (Mother), stretching her hand out.

We all look at each other and hesitantly give away our phones individually. Mamá takes it into her hands and pockets all four phones, and says, 'Please behave yourselves if you don't want to see the worst side of your Yamuna abuelita (Grandma), ' she warns us, looking at each one of us and shuts the door behind her and locks it up before she leaves.

'Woah, that was not like her.' says Sameeksha, almost suspicious.

'What else can she do, apart from warning us.' continues Aarav.

'That's true. She is concerned about us.' I say.

'Guys, I am genuinely sorry. I promise you three that I will make up for this, but I must go now. This is my only chance. Please help me.' says Dhruv pleading with us.

'If you had not put on a show, Aarav and GG would have met the contractor and Maneeksha, and I would have tried to find something about Yamuna abuelita (Grandma).' says Sameeksha with a down heart.

'I said, I am sorry, Sam. I promise I will never do such a thing again.' says Dhruv regretting what he has done.

'Okay now, enough of your sorries. Whatever happened has happened, we can't do anything about it. Now, Let's focus on how we can escape this situation.

'We must help GG.' I say.

'We shall first think of a plan to sneak Dhruv out of this house and then stick to our strategy of helping GG as planned.' says Aarav.

'Alright, let us look around the room so we may find something or devise a plan.' says Sameeksha, for which the three of us nod our heads in agreement.

The four of us walk in four directions.

I look around the room. There are no windows, just blaring artificial light that makes you squint. The walls were lined with trays and cupboards – I noticed gleaming stainless-steel utensils and vials of liquids. A clock ticking on one of the walls sounds eerily loud in the room's silence. In the centre of the room stands a small screen tv, with an antenna on top and a few pressable buttons on the edge of the tv frame, presumably not working.

"Guys, come here. Look at this. I found something.' says Sameeksha.

Aarav, Dhruv and I walk towards Sameeksha, who is now pointing towards the corner of a wall painted in a pattern.

'Interestingly, all the walls have the same paint colour, except for this section.' says Sameeksha with bright eyes of curiosity.

'That's weird.' I say, thinking about the odds.

'So? I don't get it.' says Dhruv scratching his chin.

Aarav walks towards the patterned wall, touches it, and says, 'You see? It's the size of an entryway, and I don't think this is a wall,'

All three of us glare at him, 'Won't believe me? Look at this,' says Aarav and knocks on the wall.

Rat-tat-tat

'Sí, that sound. It was not a wall,' I think, almost surprised.

'Gee, whizz! You are a genius, bro.' says Dhruv with a broad smile.

Our first discovery in the basement brought a huge smile to everyone's face.

'Come on now, we must break this thing to see what is on the other side.' says Aarav.

'Okay, let's try to find any objects which can break this thing.' says Sameeksha.

'Yo!' says Dhruv with determination filled in his tone.

We split again in four directions to find a solid object to break the patterned door.

I walk towards the cupboard again and say, 'Do any of these utensils work?'

'Lol, are you serious? With utensils?' says Dhruv, mocking me.

'Come on! they are steel.' I say, rolling my eyes. I slide the cupboard to open it, quickly grab one of the liquid vials, and try to sniff it.

'Guys, look, I think this is a disinfectant liquid. We can use this if we have a lighter and set a fire.' I say with a sparkle on my face.

Aarav walks closer to me and grabs the vial from my hand to check, and looks up at the other liquid vials in the cupboard 'Good job Mannu, this will do.', says Aarav.

'Are you both kidding?' says Sameeksha. 'We can't set a fire that will vent out smoke, and how do we put off the fire after the door is burnt?' she continues.

'Exactly. Have you both lost it?' questions Dhruv.

'Hey, just a minute. Hold on to this.' says Aarav, handing me over the vial as he walks. He makes his way towards the centre of the room and stomps on the carpet, which is uneven. There was a quiver of shake and a sound which accompanied it.

Sameeksha quickly walks towards Aarav and tries to lift the carpet with Dhruv's help. They pull out the rug to see an uneven tile on the floor. We all gather around the tile and try to remove the tile when a knock on the door stops us.

The four of us look at each other's faces. Sameeksha and I quickly tried to set the carpet while Aarav and Dhruv put the vial back inside the cupboard and pretended we were not digging any pit.

15

GG

A cluster of thoughts kept me occupied as I saw how Dhruv retaliated. 'You shouldn't have told the kids.' the back of my head screams.

At that very instance, I felt very hopeless. I could have gone and stopped the fight, the battle which Dhruv started, but if I did, the attention would have turned towards me, which would have affected the kids a lot. Yamuna would have taken that as a cue and no longer let the kids contact me. I am okay with that decision because I wanted the kids to stay out of this. It is safer that way. But what about the kids? Will they stay away from me? Or will they stop helping me if I ask them to stop? Won't they suffer mentally knowing their family is tangled in thorns?

Nevertheless, all of my great-grandchildren are very courageous and determined. They can go to any extent to save their family. Who in this world has such a great bonding with their great grandma in this generation?

Talking about the era, is it the fast-growing generation making the young kids belittle the elders for their incompetent technical knowledge, or is it simply poor parenting?

I could think of a quote in which Socrates, a Greek philosopher, once said, 'The children now love luxury;

they have bad manners; contempt for authority; they show disrespect for elders and love chatter in place of exercise. Children are now tyrants, not the servants of their households. They no longer rise when elders enter the room. They contradict their parents, chatter before company, gobble up dainties at the table, cross their legs, and tyrannise their teachers.'

I have passed through 4 generations now, and be it the technically developed generation or the advanced culture, kids are downplaying older people because of parenting. In our era, children used to stick to the morals and discipline set in the house. But nowadays, they do not abide by most of the morals. Mostly they are not aware of how older adults are treated. Though there is so much technological advancement that the parents themselves spare very little time spent with their children, the child hardly gets to see their grandparents because of the nuclear family notion.

How will the child understand the importance of family ethics, discipline or the knowledge the older people hold? Who is to be blamed? Is it the generation that has turned the children insensitive to old-aged people? Is it the parents who do not spend time with their children to teach them good or bad? Or is it just the generation which has simply changed the children with technological advancement?

But in my case, it's quite the opposite. My kids, who know me very well and are old enough to understand my phase, showed a ton of difference towards me as I aged, but on the other hand, my great-grandchildren, who knew nothing about me but stood by me with all the love and respect. I am glad I have precious little tots who respect and love me to the core. I can't let them suffer with punishments because of me. I will have to do something. I keep thinking as I watch everyone from upstairs.

'I will soon put a full stop to all of this.' I say as I watch Yamuna with fierceness in her eyes, shouting at Meenakshi.

I quickly go into my room to grab the phone. 'It's not here,' I said as I checked the lamp table. I check under my pillow and pull out the bed sheet covers. 'Where is it?' I say as I step back, thinking about checking under the bed. As I set my foot behind, I accidentally stepped on the Television remote which turned the TV on.

I bent down to grab the TV remote, as I picked up the TV remote and turned towards the TV. I tried to turn the TV off, but the remote didn't work. I smack the remote twice onto my left hand and then try pressing the power off button—still the same.

'Uff, now you even have to trouble me, is it?' I say to the remote, almost frustrated.

Nothing more can be done, so I walk towards the TV, smacking the remote. As I got closer, I noticed a news channel playing, with a wealthy middle-aged man talking while he pointed out the glass painting. Right next to him was the TV anchor, who was nodding his head. 'It's beautiful,' I say, looking at the painting. I admired the painting for some time and returned to my TV remote smacking. That's when I felt like I saw something that was familiar. I tried to get even closer to the TV.

I couldn't believe what I was seeing. "Is this for real?" I say as I rub my eyes and nod my head. 'This is real,' I say, placing a hand on my mouth in disbelief as I see the loud key in the display behind this beautiful glass painting.

I quickly move around to capture this on my phone. I move left and right, trying to find my phone. 'There…

there it is,' I say as I grab my phone under the carpet on which we sat earlier.

I hastily snapped pictures and waited patiently for the program's details until my misfortune knocked on my door. Power cut. 'Ow! No, no, no…' I say as I bang the TV twice to bring back the power.

I keep walking back and forth, thinking about how to get this carried from here. Now that I saw the key, a breath of relief filled my lungs. After today's incident, I decided to keep the kids away from this. So I head to the basement to let the kids hear the conclusion that I have come to, which is 'tell the kids to stay away from this.'

I swiftly sneak into the living room to grab the basement keys to the room. *Knock Knock Knock* I knock three times and then start unlocking the door to get inside the room in a rush. I find all four of them sighing with relief.

'Phew, GG! It's you,' says Dhruv trying to relax.

'GG!' says Sameeksha and Maneeksha, running towards me and hugging me.

'What a relief to see you here,' says Aarav with a smile.

'Come with us, GG.' says Maneeksha. 'We have something to show you.' continues Sameeksha, while both take my hand and pull towards them as if taking me somewhere.

'What's the matter?' I say, almost confused.

'How did you come here, GG? It will become a problem if anyone sees you here.' says Dhruv with concern.

'Don't worry, everything is under control,' I say and continue after a pause, 'And… I have concluded that I no longer want to involve the four of you in any of this,' I say.

Sameeksha and Maneeksha let go of my hand. 'WHAT?' questions Sameeksha and Maneeksha at a time, almost alarmed.

'Why did you say that, GG? What made you say such a thing?' questions Dhruv with a frown.

'You are not the one to be asking the question after all that you did.' says Aarav folding his arms.

Aarav then walks towards me, holds my hands and says, 'GG, I completely understand that you are concerned about us, but I want to let you know that this is not something we can blind eye to.' says Aarav, puffing out a breath.

'We want to be there for you, GG, and our family,' says Sameeksha.

'Not just for you and our family, it is also for our ancestors,' continues Maneeksha.

'It's our birthright to protect our family,' says Dhruv with much emphasis and hits the wall beside him.

All of us look at Dhruv for a brief second. Dhruv looks at everyone, lets out a nervous laugh, and continues, 'I am sorry and regretting everything that I did… And… And… I also know that I am the reason for you to think this way. I promise I won't repeat such a thing.' says Dhruv regretting.

'No, no, you're not the reason. I am just concerned about you all. You see, you keep getting punishments… And I am concerned about how this is going to affect you mentally. That's why I came to this decision. I don't want any of you hurt because of this,' I say.

'Come on, GG, we can't fight Yamuna abuelita (Grandma) if we are not together,' says Maneeksha.

'That's true, GG. We must have each other's back and stand by one another,' continues Sameeksha.

I become hesitant and keep thinking when all four gather around me.

'GG, trust us, no matter what, we will get back the key, our rituals and figure out what Yamuna abuelita's (Grandma's) mystery is,' says Dhruv.

I hug him, and everyone falls on him and hugs me in return. We stayed in that group hug for a few seconds.

I pull out from that hug and kiss all of them on their foreheads. 'I am lucky I have great-grandchildren like you,' I say as tears fill my eyes.

'We are lucky to have you, GG,' says all of them in unison and smiles back at me.

'GG!' says Maneeksha, almost excited. I turned towards her to see the eagerness on her face, 'We discovered an entryway right in that corner, and we have something hidden under this carpet,' she continued pointing out the door and stomping. 'It must be something Yamuna abuelita (Grandma) must be hiding,' she adds.

'I know what is under the carpet, and that entryway is the connection to the room adjacent to this,' I say.

'Really?! What is in the other room and this thing under the carpet makes me curious,' says Sameeksha.

'Yeah, I am curious too.' says Dhruv.

'What is in it, GG? Shall we open it up?' says Aarav looking into my eyes.

'Sure, but before I tell you what is in it... there is something else I want to show you guys.' I say as I pull out my phone.

I unlock my phone, open up the gallery and then stretch my hands to showcase what I have within the phone. 'Look at this carefully,' I say as I show them the photo on my phone.

With razor-sharp vision, all four of them now glare at my phone. 'Damn, no way!! I missed it. Now there is no way for me to go,' says Dhruv.

'Shut up, Dhruv! We are trying to focus,' says Aarav.

'You don't get it! This is my friend Yash's papá (Father). This is the secret antique library that he holds. As said, he is hosting a show before he hands over his antiques to an exhibit community,' says Dhruv with disappointment all over his face, continuing, 'for which Yash invited me before they host a TV show.'

'Is this your friend's papá?' I enquire while I zoom in on the photo.

'Sí, GG, why do you ask? There is no scope of me going there now.' says Dhruv frowning.

'Not just you; all of us have to go,' I say as I zoom in and out into the key and show all four of them.

'Wait... Wait.. wait,' says Sameeksha, taking the phone into her hands while the rest gather around Sameeksha to get a better look.

'Is this key that we are searching for?' says Maneeksha astonished.

'No way!' says Aarav, running his hands through his hair.

'Show me.' says Dhruv, taking the phone from Sameeksha's hands.

'Sí, that is our key.. Our ancient laud key,' I say, nodding.

'This is unbelievable!' says Dhruv, letting out a laugh.

'How is that even possible, GG?' questions Sameeksha out of curiosity. I shrug, not knowing the facts.

'Ay, Dios mío, I can't believe this. We located the key.' says Maneeksha, jumping with excitement.

'GG, this is blowing my mind away. We need to take custody of that key right away,' says Aarav.

'Sí, but where is this located? How do we get inside that place? And most importantly, how do we take its custody?' I say, taking my phone from Dhruv's hands.

'Come on, GG; this is way too easy for us. I know that guy in the photo; he is my friend Yash's papá (Father), and that place is Yash's house,' says Dhruv with a weird laugh.

'Don't be silly, Dhruv. We know that person is your friend's papá (Father), but it's not like he will give us the key when we ask him,' says Maneeksha.

'And how will anyone believe that the key is ours? We must tell them the story behind the key and the box as proof to gain their trust. And who will believe that story anyway?' says Sameeksha.

'That's true, Sam. No one will ever believe in that story,' says Aarav.

We all remain silent as we think of a way to get hold of our key.

'The only way we have right now,' says Dhruv with a pause, looking at all our faces… and continuing, 'is to rob the key!'

16

DHRUV

'Whattt! Have you lost it, Dhruv?' says Maneeksha.

'No way!! We are robbing,' says Sameeksha.

'How did you even come up with that thought,' says Aarav.

The three of them say back to back, and GG, on the other hand, stays quiet, trying to sink in the words I just spoke.

'Come on, you all!!' I say, rolling my eyes and going on, 'It's no big deal. We are just taking back what is ours.' I say.

Everyone stays quiet, looking at each other's faces. 'Whatt.. come on, we have no other way apart from this.' I say, trying to encourage everyone to a race we never participated in.

'Dhruv is right. I think I am in,' says Maneeksha and walks over to me.

'Mannu… come to your senses,' says Sameeksha, in shock as Maneeksha walks over to me.

'No, Sam, I am in my senses. Just think about it. What choice do we have?' questions Maneeksha.

'Sí, what choice do we have apart from this? Can any of you come up with a better idea than this?' I question, looking at Sameeksha and Aarav.

Aarav and Sameeksha look at each other for a few seconds and nod in disagreement to state that they do not have any other ideas.

'Wait, this is not our decision. Let's ask what GG thinks about this,' says Aarav, and we all look at GG for an answer.

GG remains still and sighs.

'You see, kids, We all can do noble or terrible things. The side of the equation we end up on depends on our decisions, not the condition in which we find ourselves. In simple terms, If we try to eliminate one wave with another, we end up with an infinite sea,' says GG.

'That makes sense, GG, but why do you think we will repeat the same mistake?' says Dhruv, stretching his head.

'Okay, I understand this is the only way, but what guarantees we won't get caught?' questions Sameeksha.

'That... that... I am not sure. It all depends on how we plan,' I say.

'It's not just about planning. It's also about executing it properly,' says Aarav and continues, 'Alright, let's say we have agreed on the robbery... How will you plan one without getting caught,'

'Hmm... Well, I haven't come up with a plan yet, but one thing is for sure I can gather information from my friend Yash, and based on that, we can think of a plan.' I say with quite a lot of determination.

'Sí, that's an advantage,' says Maneeksha, backing me up.

Another pause from everyone until Aarav breaks the silence, 'GG, I think we have to club hands now. There is no better way than to rob,' says Aarav.

'Sí, GG, even I feel the same.' says Sameeksha.

'Well, if it is that way, we need to follow a few sets of obligations-

'Firstly, our primary motto is to avoid getting caught. Secondly, we not only need to have proper planning but also proper execution. And, finally, it's a wide range of library, so a key missing is relatively not an unnoticeable thing as it is an antique, so we must make sure to replace our key with a dummy not to grab any focus on us,' says GG, looking at all the four of us.

'Sí, GG, we will keep that in mind and work accordingly,' says Aarav.

We all nod our heads in agreement.

'MISSION IMPOSSIBLE it is,' says Maneeksha with a glowing determination.

'Sí, Mission Impossible it is,' says GG with a smile, and we all club our hands together.

'So, where do we start now?' questions GG.

'Well, firstly, we need to figure out a way to get out of this basement and get hold of our phones so that Dhruv will get in touch with his friend to know more details, based on which we can plan,' says Maneeksha.

'Alright! Let's start working on it,' says Aarav.

'Wait, before that, I have to show you something else,' says GG, looking at the carpet and walking towards it. 'Can any of you help me lift this?' she continues while picking up the rim of the carpet.

Aarav and I rush towards the carpet. I take the rim of the carpet that GG is holding, and Aarav holds the other edge as we lift it away. Sameeksha and Maneeksha pull out the tile as GG walks towards it.

GG squats and stretches one of her arms into the pit-like gap formed from removing the tile. She then looks into the pit as if searching for something.

It looks like it is a deeply dug trench, which is pitch dark. I quickly go towards her and double-tap on my smartwatch for the light. 'GG, you can use this,' I say, proud of my watch.

'Ah, that works. Why don't you grab the thing inside this shaft?' says GG.

I kneel on the floor and bend as my hands descend into the shallow pit. 'I can feel something,' I say, looking at GG.

'Alright, pull it out. Careful, it's a little heavier, so use both hands,' says GG.

I nod, quickly sink in my other hand, grab a grip around a handle-like thing, and pull it out.

Everyone, along with me, was amused to see this beautiful ancient-looking lacquered box as I pulled it out from the shaft.

'Ay, Dios mío, this looks terrific,' says Maneeksha with an unbelievable expression.

Sameeksha and Aarav, on the other hand, couldn't speak a word as they were awed.

GG quickly grabs from my hands as I get up and stand on my feet.

'So kids, this is the lacquered box. It is not just a box but a relic of our family,' GG gleamingly says. She then points at the carving at the bottom of the box and continues, 'All these people carved are long gone, yet they are still here, enigmatic yet intact and oddly robust. This is our pride. We have to keep it and cherish it by passing it to the next generations by keeping it in the family,' she says with a smile.

We all smile back with gleaming pride in our eyes. 'This relic of ours will sustain in this family, passing on from generation to generation no matter what,' says Aarav.

'And we will be carved just like our ancestors,' I say.

'GG, how does this work, though?' questions Sameeksha.

'Yeah, I was about to ask the same question, how does it work? I don't see the keyhole on this box,' says Maneeksha.

GG pointed out the four-digit numbers on the bottom edge of the box. 'You see these numbers? Once we arrange the correct order of numbers, these four numbers split into a portion of two digits, so… these two digits slide to the right while the other two digits slide to the left, revealing the keyhole,' says GG explaining the workaround.

'Wow, this is so fascinating. It is just like the in-built number lock suitcase,' says Aarav.

'But, unbelievably, this has double security,' adds Sameeksha.

'Yeah, you not only have to get the passcode number right, but you must also have the key to open it. This is brilliant,' says Maneeksha.

'People in those days are more intelligent than us,' I add.

'Well, you can say so… this box is ages old,' says GG.

'But GG, this question remains in my head, how did it get into our family?' I ask out of curiosity.

'This ancient lacquer box and the laud key were passed on to us by my suegra (Daughter-in-law) by her papá (Father). My Suegra's papá (Daughter-in-law's father) ran a trauma cleaning service in Mexico. Back then, trauma cleaning was crucial, and the people believed it's not ordinary to take up this profession,' says GG when Maneeksha interrupts.

'What is this trauma cleaning service? Why is it considered a crucial part?' Maneeksha asks questions with a visible question mark.

'Trauma cleaning service means providing cleaning service for traumatic incidents. In other words, the trauma cleaners clean up the area where the deceased person dies,' says GG and gives a pause.

'I never heard of such a thing before. Does this exist even now?' I question out of curiosity.

'For sure, it does, but back in those days in Mexico, people considered this a crucial service because there was not much technology as we do now, and, besides that, Mexicans believe the trauma cleaners are the soul connectors after death as they read the deceased soul. Hence, they consider this job to be respectful,' says GG.

'Ooh, I see,' says Sameeksha unconsciously as she sinks into the story as everyone does.

'So, as a trauma cleaner, my suegra´s papá (Father) was a very blizzard person; his connection with the deceased soul is considered pure as his senses of analysing the dead mind or the thoughts while they died are at a different level,' continues GG.

'Then he must have been the best traumatic cleaner on demand,' says Aarav's pride reflected in his little smile.

'Oh Sí, undoubtedly he was the number one traumatic cleaner.' GG smiles and continues, 'So, just like another day, he receives a letter for trauma cleaning services, but this letter is a little weird.'

'Weird?' I question.

'Yes, the letter stated the reward for trauma cleaning is not money but a fortune,' says GG and gives a pause.

'You see, kids, my suegra´s papá (Daughter-in-law's Father) never waited for the money he got from this service. His main motive was always to help the soul have a final departure. So he visited for the cleaning service of a man who died a mysterious death. After cleaning, an old man approached him, handed over this ancient lacquer box and the laud key, and said, "This box belongs to you. The man who died wanted you to have this." And he vanished from there,' says GG.

'Whatt?' questions Maneeksha with her jaw-dropping.

'How did he vanish? Who was he?' questions Sameeksha.

'We are not aware of it to date,' says GG, shrugging.

'This is beyond belief,' says Aarav.

All the four of us look at each other in disbelief. While we are all lost in connecting the dots, a loud knock on the door distracts us.

'Oh no, GG, you must hide,' I say out loud as my heart skips a beat.

AARAV

'What is happening here?' questions Yamuna abuelita (Grandma) in disbelief as she sees GG alongside us and then turns back, looking at Meenakshi tía, who has tagged along with her to check on the four of us.

Meenakshi tía (Aunt) shrugs as if unaware of what is happening.

Yamuna abuelita (Grandma) turned back, looking at Meenakshi tía (Aunt) and entered the room. All four of us were alarmed by her entry. Not knowing how to cover up for the presence of GG, we stood there still.

'What are you doing here, mamá (Mother)? And how did you find the keys to the basement room? Meenakshi, have you not locked this room?' questions Yamuna abuelita (Grandma).

'uh-huh.. mm-mm... I locked the room, but I happened to keep the keys in the key podium,' replies Meenakshi tía with a panic-stricken voice.

'Are you serious?' Yamuna abuelita (Grandma) questions Meenakshi tía (Aunt) in disbelief.

GG cuts her off and says, 'Come on, Yamuna, that is enough. I did not know the kids were grounded,' backing up Meenakshi tía.

'Do you want me to believe that? I am well aware all five of you are accomplices to one another. Tell me, what are you all up to?' Yamuna abuelita (Grandma) questions all of us at once.

'What is meant by accomplice?' questions Dhruv, ignoring Yamuna abuelita's (Grandma's) questions.

'Dhruv!! Watch who you're talking to,' says Meenakshi tía, annoyed.

'What is it, mamá (Mother)? I don't know what an accomplice means,' says Dhruv.

'So that you know, an accomplice means a partner in crime. It's a waste of time to question your GG. Why won't any of you tell me what's happening here if you don't want your punishments to exceed and worsen?' Yamuna abuelita (Grandma) questions pointing out to Sameeksha, Maneeksha, Dhruv, and me while she glares at us.

'Well, Yamuna abuelita (Grandma).... I no longer belong to this group because they won't let me take leadership of anything or give work to this detective's brain,' says Maneeksha, frowning.

I was struck with a thunderbolt when I heard Maneeksha say that. I look at her incredibly.

'Mannu, what are you saying?' questions Sameeksha and continues, 'Abuelita (Grandma), she is the prominent leader of this gang.'

Sameeksha then turns towards me and winks. That's when I understand the show that they are trying to set.

How is that possible for these girls? They spontaneously put on a drama whenever needed. How come they come up with such ideas and jell along quickly as if everything has already been rehearsed? In this critical situation, I can't resist thinking about how a girl's brain works in this crucial situation. Girls may be fully emotion-based rather than logic-based, so they set up a little show out of nowhere. It feels like it's their habit to make events, situations, and circumstances into a melodramatic scene. It's manipulation, and it's all for seeking attention.

I nod to dust off these thoughts and focus on how to deal with this situation right now.

'Kids, don't test my patience. You guys have already put me through enough today,' says Yamuna abuelita (Grandma), almost pissed off.

'Abuelita, I will tell you what happened…' says Dhruv looking at each of us.

The look that he gave us brought chills down my spine, 'What was he doing? Is he going to blabber all that we spoke?' I think to myself and interrupt him.

'Dhruv…Dhruv… Dhruv, hold on! You have done enough for today. I will tell you what has happened.' I say, stepping on Dhruv's foot to silence him.

'Ow… Ouch! What's wrong with you, bro? Why did you step on my feet?' yells Dhruv in pain, while he leaps on one foot and continues, 'Abuelita, it was me… It was me who texted GG,' says Dhruv.

In distrust, Yamuna abuelita (Grandma) looks at Meenakshi tía (Aunt) and questions, 'Have you not confiscated their phones?'

Before Meenakshi tía answers, Dhruv goes on again, 'Sí, Sí, you're right; mamá has taken all of our phones, but I texted GG from my smartwatch. GG had no idea we were grounded, so I just passed on the information that we are being high and dry in the basement. That's all.' says Dhruv, shrugging.

'And, out of concern, I just came to check on them, nothing much.' says GG, looking at us.

'Meenakshi!! Come here right away. Why don't you do your job correctly?' Yells Yamuna abuelita (Grandma) at Meenakshi tía (Aunt).

We all looked at each other then and felt very sorry for Meenakshi tía (Aunt). We have put her through a lot today because of us; she is in a whammy situation.

'I am sorry. I was unaware they had this facility to communicate through a smartwatch. I will take the watches away right now,' says Meenakshi tía (Aunt), walking towards us.

'Also, don't give them dinner today as a punishment, and mamá (Mother), now that you know they are punished, I don't want to see you around the kids. If not, their punishment will be increasing daily,' warns Yamuna abuelita (Grandma), walks out the door, and stops there for a second.

'Also, lock the door before leaving this room and keep the keys with you along with their smartwatches and phones,' Yamuna abuelita (Grandma) continues and goes from there.

Meenakshi tía (Aunt) nods in agreement and stands there still. When Yamuna abuelita (Grandma) leaves, she walks to us to collect the smartwatches.

While she got closer to Dhruv, I noticed that she had her phone in the front pocket of the apron that she was wearing. I gesture to Sameeksha and Maneeksha with my eyes, pointing out the phone.

Meenakshi tía (Aunt) is a part of Dhruv's school classmate's WhatsApp group. So, I firmly believe we can fetch Yash's number from that.

As soon as I gestured, they both immediately understood, and as easy as a piece of cake, they quickly abducted the phone while Dhruv was pleading and apologising to Meenakshi tía.

'I did not expect this from you, Dhruv. You clubbed your hands with these two wicked-minded girls who turned you into this.' says Meenakshi with anger as she collects our smartwatches.

'Alright then, I will be leaving now. Good night kids.' says GG gesturing for us to call her on the phone.

Dhruv and I give her a thumbs up while Sameeksha and Maneeksha shout out "good night, GG, sleep well" with a wink.

GG leaves, and right after that, Meenakshi tía (Aunt) goes from there, locking us in the room.

'Well… what now?' questions Dhruv.

'You call your friend Yash from mamá's phone and try to fetch some details of the key's whereabouts,' says Maneeksha while Sameeksha hands him the phone.

'Okay, I will do it right away,' says Dhruv as he takes the phone and moves towards a corner of the room.

'Now, how do we get out of here?' I question, looking at Sameeksha and Maneeksha.

'Before we start getting busy finding a way, why don't we check that patterned door until Dhruv returns from the call? What say?' says Sameeksha raising her eyebrows up and down.

'Yeah, how can we forget that? Let's get into it,' says Maneeksha in agreement.

We walk towards the door when Sameeksha jumps with the idea, 'Hey! Why don't I use that tile?'

'Yeah, that would work.' I say as I walk towards the carpet and pull out the uneven tile.

'Alright, on the count of three, go for it.' says Maneeksha.

'Ready....1 .... 2..... 3..... GO!' says Sameeksha and Maneeksha in unison.

I displayed my potential all at once, but it did not go through the first time. I am sure this will work, but I was also concerned that this tile might break from the force. As I go for another try, Dhruv stops me.

'Wait, wait, wait, I think you should try this.' says Dhruv handing me over the fire extinguisher.

'Oh wow, Dhruv, good job.' says Sameeksha.

I take the fire extinguisher and shatter the patterned door with one hit. I keep putting my strength at once and make a wider opening for us to enter.

'I think this will do,' says Maneeksha.

The entry was very dark, so I told them, 'I will get in first, then you can follow me.'

I stepped into the room and collided with an object that seemed vaguely like a box, or that's what I assumed. The room was bleak, cold and completely dark. It was quiet and sad there, and I felt a chill as the darkness engulfed me. It was the most piercing darkness ever-it was not merely the darkness that came out of the absence of light; it was much more sinister.

The pitch-black atmosphere was impenetrable, and I stood rooted to the spot, trying to stretch my eyes as wide as possible, but I could barely make out a feeble outline of some distant object. There was nothing warm about this place. It smelled of something evil, and the darkness was surreal. Cold and clammy, I tried to creep out, but it was futile. I was neither in nor out-too terrified to move lest I make a loud racket.

The darkness and quiet pressed into my ears, and I drew out a chilling scream that seemed to warm my lungs with an inhuman warmth in the overwhelming darkness…

'What is it, bro?' questions Dhruv.

'Nothing, it's too dark in here.' I screamed as it felt like I was trapped in a bubble without an exit until it popped out.

'Hold on, we are coming.' says Sameeksha, entering the doorway.

'Dhruv, hand us over the phone, and you stay here.' says Maneeskha.

Dhruv nods in agreement and hands them over the phone. Maneeksha turns on the torch light and hands it over to Sameeksha.

'Vintage-styled place.' says Sameeksha as she walks into the passage.

'GG told us this entryway connects to the next door,' replies Maneeksha.

As they flash the torch across the room, the tiny ray of light hits my face as it passes.

'Sam, this way. I am right here,' I call out to them and continue, 'This place is creepy. I don't get a good vibe from here.'

'Yeah, I feel it too.' says Maneeksha.

'Sam, don't leave me like that... This darkness is running chills down my spine… Sam... Sam! Where are you?' questions Maneeksha with fright in her voice.

I saw Maneeksha's face through the flashlight and started walking towards her, saying, 'Sameeksha, don't move the flashlight. I am walking in the direction of Maneeksha.'

Sameeksha reached out to Maneeksha, flaring the light towards her direction, making it easy for both of us to walk towards her.

'Alright now, we shall all stick together until we find a source of light. This torch light is no help.' says Sameeksha as we grab each other's hands.

'Here, hand me over the phone,' I say as I take over the phone and point the torch downwards, sideward in slow motion.

'There... There... There....' says Maneeksha pointing towards the sidewalk, 'I saw something like a spark.' she continued.

'Yeah, I think I saw it, too.' says Sameeksha.

'Me too! Let us see what it is,' I say as we start walking towards the spark.

Walking towards the spark, we understand it's an electric spark from a vintage-styled toggle light switch.

'How do we turn on this thing now?' questions Sameeksha.

'Wait, I think we can make use of our footwear.' I say and continue, 'Mannu, give me the slippers you wear,'

'What, why mine? You already have yours.' says Maneeksha.

'Come on, Mannu, yours is made of rubber.' says Sameeksha.

'Alright, fine. Here you go.' says Maneeksha handing over her slippers to me.

'Thanks!' I say and try to turn on the toggle light switch with Maneeksha's slipper.

It was still dark. Nothing changed. We gave it a few seconds and waited. And, there it was... The lights started to blink two or three times and finally ignited the room.

The view that we had not only amused us but also brought goosebumps all over our bodies while our knees got weak and our legs gave up to stand still. We couldn't believe what we were seeing.

'What is all this? Who are all these people?' says Sameeksha, stepping forward with her jaw open.

We were surrounded by a room filled with paintings of people. The paintings have exquisite details and are so realistic, as if the people in the photo are real and are watching us.

'What the hell! This looks so realistic,' mutters Maneeksha in disbelief.

'I walk towards one of the paintings; the person in the painting is real, in the arts, the accurate, detailed, unembellished depiction of nature or contemporary life. They say a painting is worth a thousand pictures, and these realistic portraits are so lively causing brain fog. It's more or less like a 3D portrait painting. I assume the artist to be a human camera with excellent skills to duplicate reality onto the canvas. These realistic portraits are not just a visual representation of the person who has been painted but also reveal something about the person's essence.

These intense portraits captivate us, draw us towards the painting, and make us wonder about the person depicted. Are these paintings a biography? Did the artist carefully craft visual clues to tell the person's story in the artwork?

'No way this is real!' says Dhruv, distracting everyone in the room. 'Is this for real?' he continues towards one of the paintings.

'This has no artist name.' says Dhruv pointing out the painting.

'I guess none of these paintings have the artist's name on them,' I say.

"Guys, look at this painting," says Maneeksha, pointing out one of the paintings of a woman at the centre of the room.

I turn towards Maneeksha to look at the painting. The painting, which she pointed out, is a little wider than the other paintings in the room and is placed in the centre of the room, while all the other paintings are sideways, fully covered from left to right.

The painting portrays a woman's face, capturing a duality of emotions and contrasting energies. The artist skillfully draws her features into two halves, each representing a contrasting emotional state.

On one side of the woman's face, an expression of radiant happiness radiates. Her eyes sparkle joyfully, and her lips curve into a gentle smile. This side of her face is bathed in warm, vibrant colours, portraying a sense of lightness and fulfilment. It reflects moments of bliss, calm, and the beauty of life's brighter aspects.

However, the other half of her face tells a different story. Here, a profound sadness lingers. Her eyes, filled with a hint of sorrow, gaze into the distance. Her lips turn downwards, subtly revealing the weight of her inner pain. This side of her face is cloaked in cooler, muted tones, suggesting a sense of melancholy and introspection. It captures the depths of her emotions, the trials she has faced, and the challenges she carries within.

Behind the woman, a black, shadowy figure with piercing red eyes looms sinisterly. The figure represents a haunting presence or a symbol of the woman's inner turmoil. Its presence evokes a sense of mystery, darkness, and the struggles hidden beneath the surface. The contrast between the woman's dual emotions and the enigmatic figure accentuates the complexity and depth of her emotional journey.

The overall composition creates a visual tension between opposing emotions, inviting viewers to reflect on the multifaceted nature of human experiences. The painting is a powerful exploration of the coexistence of happiness and sadness, light and darkness, and the intricate interplay between our emotions and the shadowy depths of our psyche. It invites contemplation and encourages viewers to explore their emotional complexities and introspections.

'This looks a little odd from the other paintings, right,' says Sameeksha, walking towards the painting.

'Woww! The woman in the painting is so beautiful. I did not find anything odd in this painting except that this is placed at the centre and is a little wider than other paintings,' says Dhruv.

'Exactly, that is why the question arises. Why is this painting different from others?' says Sameeksha.

I walk closer towards the painting to observe the detailing of the painting. 'They say an artwork can speak a hidden language. If we watch closely, this art may reveal some answers,' I say.

Sameeksha, Maneeksha and Dhruv get closer to the painting. The most evident detailing is the thinnest line which separates the painting into two halves. The line is so thin that you can only notice it when you get closer.

'Look at this thin line across the painting,' I say as I point it out.

'And also this, the right-side eye of this painting is filled with sorrow,' says Dhruv, moves towards the left side, and says, 'this side of the eye is different… it is happy.'

'I think this thin line across the painting is to differentiate the happy and sad face,' says Sameeksha, looking at the painting.

'Oh my, I am curious about the artist who painted this. The detailing is so nanoscopic yet very beautiful,' says Maneeksha, mesmerised by the painting.

'Yeah, I also can't stop thinking about who these people are. Who painted them so realistically? Why are these in the basement? And why is this painting so different from the rest?' says Sameeksha, pointing out the artwork in the centre of the room.

'Whatsoever, this is the most beautiful painting I have ever seen,' says Dhruv, resting his face with closed eyes, almost hugging it.

'Dhruv, step back. Don't touch it,' says Maneeksha while Sameeksha tries to pull him by his hand.

'Hold on, let me just…' says Dhruv, opening his eyes and getting closer to the painting again. 'Wait, wait, wait… There is a line here,' continues with Dhruv and gets a closer look at it.

'Guys, this line is not a part of the painting!' says Dhruv looking into it and continues, 'Pass me the phone torch.'

'Here you go,' I say as I quickly pull out the phone from my pocket, turn on the torch and hand it over to Dhruv.

Dhruv takes the phone and passes the torch through the thin line. 'Nothing is visible,' says Dhruv.

'Come on!' says Maneeksha and bangs on the painting twice and continues, 'I thought we found a clue,' says Maneeksha, disappointed.

'Mannu, no, why did you have to bang the painting!' says Sameeksha with shock.

'Guys, did you notice this?' says Dhruv.

'This thin line got a little wide.' I say, observing the now visible slit on the painting.

'Oh! Is it?' says Maneeksha stunned, 'I think we need to bang this thing more,' she continues.

THUD THUD THUD THUD

Sameeksha, Maneeksha, and I bang on the painting.

'This is working,' says Dhruv, jumping with excitement.

I take the phone from Dhruv and flash the light across the opening between the paintings while Sameeksha and Maneeksha continue banging.

'Guys, I see a passage with a ladder,' I say and continue, 'Let me see if I can fit into this,' I say as I try to get through.

'I think you are a little big to fit into this. Let me try,' says Maneeksha, squishing herself inside and grabbing the phone from my hand.

With quite a lot of excitement, she moves the ladder upward, and we all wait for a minute when we hear her excitement-filled muffled voice.

'Guys! We made it! This takes us to the backyard,' says Maneeksha.

YAMUNA

April 22nd 1977 - 2 am

I snap open my eyes, my body covered in cold sweat, shaking, heart pounding, looking around the room, suspicious and paranoid that the horror may have followed me here. I get up cautiously, shivering, rubbing my head and my eyes. I take a few breaths and stumble to the bathroom, looking into the mirror slowly and cautiously, unsure what I'll see in the reflection.

I look at myself, drenched in sweat. I quickly splash some water on my face to wash away the traces of the horror, leaving me relieved. I walk back to my bed and lay my head on my pillow, eyes wide open, looking at the ceiling. I kept going back and forth, trying to figure out what was chasing me in my nightmare, which I just had.

It was the dead of the night, the clock striking 2:30 a.m., when I heard an urgent knocking on my door. Startled, my heart raced with anticipation and curiosity. A sense of recognition coursed through me, and I swiftly opened the door with trembling hands. My dear tío Narendra (Uncle) stood before me, his face etched with fear and concern.

Narendra's (Uncle) arrival at such an hour sent shivers down my spine, for I could see the lingering effects of a chaotic nightmare still haunting him. The intensity of his gaze held a depth of understanding as if an otherworldly revelation had touched him. The dream had unearthed a foreboding sense, a premonition of impending doom that chilled him to the core.

'Yamuna… are you okay?' says Narendra tío (Uncle), worried. I have never seen him this worried before.

'I am okay, tío (Uncle). Why are you up at this hour? What's wrong?' I ask tío (Uncle) out of concern.

Narendra tío (Uncle) keeps breathing heavily, huffing and puffing, and speaking is almost difficult.

'Come on in. Have a seat here,' I say, guiding him towards my study chair and making him sit.

'Stay here. I will get you some water,' I say to him and head towards the kitchen.

As I turn around to leave, Narendra tío (Uncle) quickly grabs my wrist. 'No, just stay with me,' he says.

'Tío (Uncle), what happened? You are panicking me,' I say, looking into his eyes.

'Promise me, whatever I am saying now should be between us,' says Narendra tío (Uncle).

I nod my head in agreement.

'I got an indication something terrible will happen to you. I don't know how or what, but something will happen,' says Narendra tío (Uncle) with trembling fright.

'Come on, tío (Uncle), what evil will happen to me when you are around? How sure are you about this? And what kind of Indication? and How?' I questioned him in disbelief.

'This is serious. I had a nightmare in which I happened to paint. And I painted a portrait of you with a significant difference on either side of the face which caught me off guard,' says tío (Uncle) with worry in his voice.

'Nightmare? What did you see in your nightmare? And what made you paint my portrait?' I question, trying to sink in the information.

'I... Uh.. mm… I can hardly not make out what kind of nightmare it was. It was more like an intense fear which rushed through me while having this nightmare, indicating something terrible. And in that trance, my hand was urged to paint the bits and pieces of the nightmare which turned out to be your portrait,' says Narendra tío (Uncle) at one stretch.

'I guess just the feeling of the nightmare might have got you worried, and What could be so wrong? It's just my portrait.' I say, almost carefree, but deep down, I know something is off.

'No, you don't understand. I never painted anyone's portrait except for our ancestors, whom I see on Día de los Muertos. And your portrait is not like a regular portrait. It has happiness on one side, and the other side has terrific sorrows.'

With concern engraved on his face, Narendra tío (Uncle) turned to me, his voice filled with fear and urgency. He had come to my room, driven by an instinctive need to ensure my safety and well-being. The nightmare had stirred within him a fear that something threatening loomed on the horizon, and he couldn't bear the thought of leaving those he cherished vulnerable to its close threat.

'I had a very chaotic nightmare from which I hastily rose. I couldn't sink in or describe what I saw, so my hands were responsible for painting it. To my astonishment, it was the exact image that had haunted my dream—the portrait of you split between happiness and sadness… and… and… Behind you a shadowy figure hiding, its piercing red eyes casting an unsettling aura,' says Narendra tío (Uncle).

He was lost in his thoughts while he kept explaining his nightmare with intensity.

'Gazing at the painting I drew within a matter of minutes, I couldn't shake the anxiety surrounding me. The familiarity of the artwork sent chills through my veins, confirming the feeling that something threatening had emerged on the horizon. The comparison of your contrasting emotions symbolised an extreme duality that echoed within me. It was as if the darkness within the painting had come to life, mirroring the threatening presence that had filled my nightmare.' Narendra tío (Uncle) continues.

Narendra Tío (Uncle) couldn't shake the intensity of the encounter, for it felt like a whispered forecast, a glimpse into a realm where dreams and reality intertwined. It felt as if he was staring at the painting in which his mind raced with questions and fears and a newfound determination to uncover the truth beyond the enigmatic brushstrokes. Deep within his soul, he knew that this painting held a hidden message, a warning of the nearing storm that awaited us.

As we stood there, wrapped in the stillness of the night, I felt a renewed sense of comfort and security. Narendra tío (Uncle)'s protective presence reminded me we were not alone in facing the unknown. United by love, we would navigate the shadows that threatened to barge upon our lives, standing faithful against the tides of uncertainty.

'I don't know where to start looking for answers,' says Narendra tío (Uncle).

'Don't worry about me tío (Uncle); nothing will happen to me. I will be safe and sound. We will figure this out together,' I say, assuring tío (Uncle).

Narendra tío (Uncle) pulls me into a hug and kisses me on the forehead, 'I will not let anything happen to you or our family,' he says and continues, 'Come on now, I will put you to bed.'

As he tucked me into the soft fold of the bed, I nestled into the embrace of the blankets, and I closed my eyes while Narendra tío (Uncle) kept patting me to sleep.

I suddenly opened my eyes with a question bobbing in my head. 'Narendra tío (Uncle), I don't understand why you have asked me to keep this a secret. Why should this be between us? Why can't I tell anyone about the nightmare or the portrait?'

'I am not sure how Mahendra Hermano would react to it. So I want this to be a secret until we discover the truth,' says Narendra tío (Uncle), lost in thought.

'Tío... I know how much you love me and how much you are worried about me. And I want you to be assured that nothing will happen to me. I promise I will never talk about this nightmare, not with anybody or even you, for that matter of fact.' I kept talking while I dozed off to sleep.

April 23rd, 1977 - Next day,

The little room feels much smaller than usual. Like something outside pressing against the windows, aching to come in; maybe it is the noise. It is probably the noise. Tap. Tap. Tap. A thousand, million taps at once. The language of water.

I can't stop thinking of Narendra tío's (Uncle's) unsettling nightmare lingering in your mind. Various possibilities and interpretations raced through your thoughts. The vivid imagery of my face with its contrasting emotions and the threatening presence of the shadowy figure with red eyes left me with unease and curiosity.

I kept pondering whether the nightmare could symbolise hidden conflicts or emotions within the family. Perhaps it hinted at suppressed tensions or unspoken secrets yet to be revealed.

My mind raced with possibilities as the mystery of the nightmare deepened, leaving me with insatiable curiosity to uncover the truth behind its symbolism and significance.

As I immersed myself in contemplation, I couldn't help but wonder if there were hidden clues within the nightmare that would eventually unravel its meaning. I vowed to stay vigilant and observant, ready to piece together the puzzle fragments before you.

In the end, only time would reveal the true nature and significance of the nightmare. Still, the lingering sense of anticipation and unease captivated my thoughts, yearning for answers and resolution to the enigmatic visions gripping Narendra tío´s (Uncle's) sleep.

I wrap myself in it, feeling surrounded and safe. Wrapped in sound as vibrant as a drum, wrapped in the cold as foreboding as stone.

'I am coming in,' says a voice.

I do not care to turn back. I stay focused, looking outside my window while lying on the bed.

'Yamuna… are you angry with your mamá (Mother),' says my mamá (Mother), walking towards me.

I stay quiet and continue looking outside the window.

'I know you are upset. Look, I brought lunch for you,' says mamá (Mother), placing the plate on the side table. She then walks towards my bed and takes a seat next to me.

Though I am upset, the delicious smell of the freshly grilled corn cob is soothing my mood.

'Won't you talk to your mamá (Mother),' says mamá (Mother), pulling me into her arms and continuing, 'See what I prepared for you. Your favourite Elote. I designed it just how you like, these corn cobs are slathered in mayo cream sauce while it's grilled, and I added the right amount of chilli powder, cheese and lime. It's delicious,' she says while she rocks me back and forth in her arms.

'Yumm, this sounds so tempting. And it feels heavenly if I have it in this weather,' I think.

My mamá (Mother) pulled me away from the hug and held my face, wiping away the hair falling on my face. 'Yamuna, I am sorry for yelling at you. I am concerned about my hija because I love her so much,' she says, kissing me on the forehead and continuing.

'You see, if you get wet in the rain, you will get sick. And I don't want my hija (Daughter) to suffer.'

'But mamá (Mother), you know how much I love to play in the rain,' I say with a frown.

'Sí, I know and know that you love Elote. Besides, the rain will cause you harm, while Elote doesn't. I apologise for yelling at you,' says mamá (Mother) with a smile.

'Hmm... Yeah, you should not have yelled at me,' I say, smiling back at her.

'Come on now, have this Elote while it's still hot. It's lovely to eat in cold rainy weather like this,' says mamá (Mother), handing me over the plate.

I sit straight, folding my legs and taking the plate into my hands, happiness filling my eyes. I sniff the Elotes from the plate, take one into my hands and quickly bite into it, closing my eyes.

'Wow, this feels so heavenly,' I say as I chew on the corn cob.

'Here, squeeze a dashing amount of lime onto it,' says mamá (Mother), handing me over the lemon.

I squeeze in a few drops and smack my tongue, 'This is mouthwatering,' I say.

Mamá (Mother) chuckles, kisses me on my forehead, and says, 'Alright then, enjoy your Elote. I have a few chores to complete,' she says as she pats my head.

'Mmm…' I say, closing my eyes as the flavours in my mouth explode.

As I enjoy my Elote with my eyes closed, I hear another voice. It's my tío (Uncle), Narendra Varma.

'What is my little devil doing?' he says, smiling at me.

I open my eyes and offer him one of the Elotes on the plate. 'This is so tasty! Would you like some?' I say.

'Well, it's usual for people to enjoy hot snacks in this pouring weather, but people like us… want… this,' says Narendra tío (Uncle), pulling out an ice cream stick from the cover he is holding.

'Woww! Ice cream!! I love having ice creams in the cold weather,' I say as I extend my hand to take it from his hands but stop immediately.

'Come on, take it. What made you stop?' says Narendra tío (Uncle), noticing a little frown on my face.

'Mamá (Mother) yelled at me earlier not to get wet in the rain. She is worried I will catch a cold and fall sick. She will be mad at me if she learns I have an ice cream,' I say.

'Want to know something? Your mamá (Mother) is just like the regular people in the world. But us… we are different; we are unique from others… We are the kind of people who enjoy the cold shivers in the cold weather rather than looking for comforting warmth in cold weather,' says tío (Uncle), with pride in his voice and takes out the wrapper from the ice cream and hands it over to me.

'Here you go. Do what you like. Remember this, never hesitate to do something you love,' says tío (Uncle) with a smile.

'Would you like to play in the rain along with me?' I ask mischievously as I smile and take the ice cream from his hands.

'Why not?' says Narendra tío (Uncle), with a wide smile.

We both quickly start running to the terrace and get drenched in the rain while having ice cream.

'This is so fun, and ice cream makes it even better,' I say to tío (Uncle), giggling with happiness.

I played with tío for nearly 20 mins in the rain. We kept jumping, running, and spinning until the cold breeze ran shivers down our spine, bringing instant sneezes.

'Alright, I think this is enough,' says tío (Uncle).

I nod my head in agreement and make a move out of there. We both take tiny steps to ensure not to get caught by anyone. Tío (Uncle) leads the way as I hide behind him and walk in his footsteps.

'Narendra, look at you,' says papá (Father), looking at his hermano with concern.

We were caught off guard when we heard him speak. I held tío's (Uncle's) shirt from behind in fright.

'Gee, uh… Ah… I say tío (Uncle), clearing his throat. 'Yeah, I am drenched completely,' says tío (Uncle) with an awkward laugh. 'What's up, hermano?' questions tío (Uncle).

'Well, I want you to visit the post office and drop this letter,' says papá (Father), handing him over the letter.

'Ah... Ok... You want me to do it right now?' questions tío (Uncle), taking the letter into his hands.

'Yeah, it's very urgent. I know it is pouring continuously, but I am caught up with other things. You can take my car,'

'Alright, I will quickly change and head to the post office,' says tío (Uncle).

'Thank you so much!' says papá (Father) and leaves there in haste.

Tío (Father) waits until papá (Father) leaves and grabs my hand, rushing me to my room.

'Now, quickly dry yourself. I don't want you to catch a cold. And yes, you can also check out the painting in my room. I will be back in no time. And don't worry; we will try to figure out about the nightmare.' says tío (Uncle) and walks away, winking at me.

I nod in agreement and smile at him as he walks away. I shut the door and quickly grab a towel with a constant smile, thinking about how we enjoyed playing in the rain.

I quickly change and dry myself up and walk out of my room. I go towards tío's (Uncle's) room out of curiosity and eagerness to witness the painting in person. I see a canvas covered with a cloth as I enter his room.

In haste, I approached the canvas board and removed the cloth to reveal what was hiding beneath it.

'No way.' I say to myself, looking at the painting.

As I stood there, gazing at the painting that depicted my face with its contrasting emotions and the haunting presence of the shadowy figure with red eyes, a wave of shock washes over me. The artwork seemed to have captured the essence of Narendra Tío's unsettling nightmare with uncanny accuracy.

'Yamuna… Yamuna… where are you?' calls out a sobbing voice.

I quickly cover the painting as it is and rush outside the room to see my mamá (Mother) running across the corridor, panicking, crying her eyes out.

'What happened, mamá (Mother)?… What happened?' I questioned her, almost afraid.

'Narendra… Narendra… tío' she says, trying to gulp some air as she speaks while crying. 'Tío? What is it, mamá (Mother)? What happened to Narendra tío (Uncle)?' I ask as panic rushes through my body at once.

'He… he… met with an accident and…' says mamá (Mother).

SAMEEKSHA

After realising we have a way out, the four of us gather around the centre of the room and plot a plan to rob the laud key.

But my mind keeps wandering around the portraits in the basement room. How can someone paint so realistically? And most importantly, who are those people? The lady's painting in the centre is a masterpiece. But why are these hidden in the basement? It has something to do with our ancestors because of the prehistoric touch reflected in the paintings.

'Sam… sam… focus,' says Aarav.

'Ah… Yes! What did I miss?' I ask, looking at everyone.

'Come on, sis, this is not the right time to zone out like this,' says Mannu.

I nod in agreement and focus on what they are discussing.

'So, listen up, guys, we have the entire night to ourselves, and besides that, no one will come to check on us until tomorrow morning,' says Aarav.

'Yeah, you are right, Aarav. Did you inform GG we found a way out from the basement?' I ask.

'Yes, I did. GG said she would meet us in the backyard around 10 PM.' says Aarav.

'What is the time now?' questions Maneeksha.

'It's 9:30 PM', says Aarav.

"We still have 30 mins. We can devise a plan by then,' I say, trying to think of an idea.

'Dhruv, did you speak with your friend? What happened?' questions Maneeksha.

'I spoke to him, but he was disappointed I did not attend. But besides that, he said the exhibit community would be handing over the antiques tomorrow and later pass them on to a local museum,' says Dhruv.

'That means the antiques are still at Yash's place,' I question.

'Yes, that's right. But with heavy security by the exhibit community,' says Dhruv with a frown.

'Ayy, Oh Dios!! Security?' says Maneeksha, exclaiming.

'Stop knitting your brows. We are a team. MISSION IMPOSSIBLE will figure it out,' I say with a wink.

'I am sure we will. But did you hear? He just said security... Like huge hefty people guarding the antiques. How will we sneak into the house without facing them?' questions Maneeksha.

'Come on, Mannu, chill. We have Dhruv to our rescue. Dhruv will call up his friend, and he will help all of us sneak into the house,' I say, looking at Dhruv.

'No way. Yash will help me sneak into his house, but why will he allow you guys? That won't make any sense to me,' says Dhruv, trying to suppress his anxiety.

'Dhruv, we have no other way. Just do it,' says Aarav, handing him the phone.

'Here, go ahead and call him,' says Aarav.

'Okay, I will call but...?' questions Dhruv.

'Tell the truth. Maybe he will help us rob and get back our key,' says Maneeksha, leaving everyone with open mouths.

'No, Mannu, that's not a good idea. What if he won't believe that the key is ours? What if he gets scared of the robbing idea?' says Aarav.

'Hmm… then what do we do?' questions Maneeksha, rolling her eyes.

I open my mouth to shout out my idea, but an instant thought keeps my mouth sealed.

'Aarav, can you pass over the phone? I think I know what needs to be done,' I say as I reach out to take the phone from him.

'What is it? What's the matter?' questions Maneeksha, with curiosity filling up her eyes.

'Nah, nothing. Don't get so excited. I am just trying to ring some friends, so maybe they can help,' I say, trying to get sidetracked.

Maneeksha glares at me with her detective's eyes, but I play it cool to avoid getting caught.

I detach from the set of three and corner myself, ensuring I am not audible to others. Once I felt assured I was ready, I quickly opened my phone and dialled Dhruv's friend Yash from the recent log.

'Dhruv! What's the matter?' says Yash.

'Hi, Yash, Sameeksha here. Dhruv's elder sister,' I say over the phone.

'Oh, Hi! What's up?' questions Yash.

'Well… Yash… I just called to tell you something important, and Dhruv is kinda worried about asking for your help in person,' I say.

'Lol, is Dhruv that scared of me? Anyways, what's the matter?' questions Yash.

'You see, Dhruv likes you a lot, and he does not want to lose you in any given circumstances, so it's hard on him to ask for your help. But besides that, only you can help Dhruv and our entire family in this present situation,' I say, almost dragging each sentence.

'Anything serious? What's the matter, sis?' questions Yash.

'You see, Yash, we lost our ancient laud key, precious to our entire family when our great grandpa died. Without that key, we cannot celebrate Dia de los Muertos, an essential Mexican festival… Our GG discovered that our laud key is in your father's secret library of antique collections,' I say.

'Why is the key so important? And How sure are you that your key is in our antique library collection?' he asks out of curiosity.

'As I said, Dia de los Muertos is an essential festival for our family. When we lost the key, we could not celebrate this festival. And our family will be in serious trouble if we do not celebrate this festival. There are so many things Yamuna Abuela is hiding from us. We can never know the truth if we do not know this right now. Besides that, GG took a picture when the TV show was running. And she was pretty sure that the key was ours as it had a carving of a tiny Calavera on the edge of the key,' I say, explaining as much as I can.

'Yeah, no offence, but I feel Yamuna's abuelita (Grandma) has a bad influence on the entire family. By the way, Calavera? What is that?' questions Yash.

'Calavera is a structure of the human skull. We prepare sugar candy in a Calavera structure for the Dia de los Muertos festival,' I say.

'Ohh, I see...' says Yash, pausing and continuing, 'So, what is in your mind?'

'Don't freak out, but we are in a thought to rob the key because, you see, we do not have any other way. If we say the key is ours, will your father believe it or give it to us immediately? Moreover, the exhibit community people might have made a note of how many antiques are present and what different antiques are present. We are just not knowing how we can get back what was ours,' I say out at a stretch without taking a breath, afraid he would deny it, but Yash remains silent without speaking a word.

'So, Dhruv hesitates to ask you because he does not want your friendship to crash in this process. But like I said, only you can help us... Our entire family... Nevertheless, it's your call if you want to help us or not. No force... but I want to let you know we must proceed with the robbery with or without your help,' I say and puff out some breath.

'Hmm... I see,' says Yash, pausing for a while as if he is thinking something, and continues, 'Well, in that case... I can go to any extent to help my friend and his family,' says Yash with determination... 'But my only concern is about GG,' says Yash.

'Thank you so much, Yash. And what about GG?' I ask.

'You see, it's a cakewalk for me to have you all at my house in the name night out... But it will be fishy if GG tags along in the name of the night out,' says Yash.

I was pretty impressed by how Yash had already started executing the plan.

'Wow, Yash, you have already started giving work to your brain. Hmm… I get it.

Now, if we all come for a night out with GG and the next day if the key goes missing… For sure, we will be the suspects.' I say and give pause. 'Is there any other way to sneak GG into your house?'

'Wait, let me think about it. How much time do we have with us?' questions Yash.

'Well, not much… We only have this entire night. Whatever we must do, we must get it over by night,' I say.

'Okay, listen to this carefully; there are six security guards. Two guards at the gate, two at the secret library door, and two inside the secret library… So, here's what we can do… I will come and pick you all up, including GG. But GG needs to hide in the car boot. Once we all enter the house, GG can slowly sneak into my room,' says Yash.

'Do you think this will work?' I question.

'Trust me, we got this. Once we clear the security guards at the gate, it is easy for GG to sneak into my room because there are no other security guards except at the secret library,' says Yash.

'Then, what about security cameras?' I question.

'We do have security cameras everywhere. But, once we leave the car, it will be parked in the garage. Our Garage is in the basement, and there are no cameras in the garage and the lift. So, GG needs to wait until the car is parked in the garage and enter the elevator,' says Yash.

'What will happen after that?' I question.

'We will use walkie-talkies and guide GG to my room. Simple,' says Yash.

'This sounds like a plan, but I am sceptical. Also, we need to plan a robbery, too,' I say.

'Don't worry. I am with you. We will make it work,' says Yash, assuring me.

'By the way, we must follow a few obligations. Firstly, our primary motto is not to get caught. Secondly, we not only need to have proper planning but also proper execution. And, finally, it's a wide range of libraries, so a key missing is relatively not an unnoticeable thing as it is an antique, so we must make sure to replace our key with a dummy not to grab any focus on us,' I say.

'Cool, we shall plan accordingly,' says Yash.

'Okay, then. I will let the others know about our plan. You pick us up around 10:30 PM,' I say.

'Alright. Toodles!' says Yash as he disconnects the call.

I disconnect the call and walk back into the group who are still breaking their heads to devise a plan. It feels like a combination of anxiety, dread, and excitement. My palms are getting sweaty, my heart rate is increasing, and I feel a fluttery nervous stomach.

As I walk towards the group, Aarav, Maneeksha, and Dhruv stop their discussions and look towards me with curious eyes.

'What's wrong? Why is everyone staring at me like that?' I question them.

'You were on call for nearly 20 mins, and now you ask us what's wrong?' says Maneeksha, folding her arms.

'Ah, well, I was on call…' I say and stop while the phone rings in my hand. It's GG calling.

'Sí, GG,' I say as I answer the call and quickly put the call on speaker.

Aarav, Maneeksha and Dhurv gather around me to listen to the call.

'I think everyone in the house slept. Let's not waste any time,' says GG.

'Okay.' we reply in unison.

'Alright, I will meet you in the backyard then,' says GG.

'GG, I have something to say to all of you,' I say, looking at everyone.

'What is it, Sam?' questions Maneeksha.

'Well, I happened to speak with Dhruv's friend Yash. He said he would help us with the robbery,' I say.

'Whattt? Really?' says Maneeksha, almost excited.

'That's a piece of good news,' says GG.

'Nice work, Sam,' says Aarav with an unbelievable expression and a smile.

I kept my eyes locked on Dhruv. But there he was in utter shock, his jaw dropped... 'You did what?' says Dhruv finally.

'Come on, Dhruv, that's not the point. He is ready to help us with the robbery.' says Aarav, patting Dhruv's back.

'Not just that, he also devised a plan to sneak us into his house,' I say.

'Wow!! That guy must be crazy,' says Maneeksha chuckling.

Really?' says Dhruv astonished.

I nod my head while I say, 'Sí.'

'What is the plan he devised?' questions GG.

'Yeah, listen up carefully, guys... So, he will pick us up around 10:30 PM and take us to his house for a night over.' I say.

'Even GG? For a night over?' questions Aarav.

'No, GG will get into the car with us... But she will stay in the car boot. Once we pass the main gate security, the vehicle will drop us at the main door and go to the garage in the basement. Once the vehicle is parked in the garage basement, GG will get out of the car and take the lift from there.' I say,

'I have been to their house once. It's huge. But, What about the security guards and the security cameras?' questions Dhruv.

'Okay, they do not have any security cameras in the garage and lift. Yash says we can use walkie-talkies and guide GG into Yash's room. And about cameras, there are only six guards… two at the gate entrance, two at the secret library and two inside the secret library.' I say.

'It sounds like a plan. What do you say, GG?' questions Maneeksha.

'Yeah, sure, we can make it work.' says GG.

'It's 10:00 PM right now. We still have 30 mins. Let's prepare everything we will need for the robbery.' says Dhruv with determination.

We all nod in agreement looking at each other.

'Alright, GG, meet us at the backyard in 5 mins… we need to sneak into our rooms and fetch all the props we need,' I say.

'Done.' says GG while she disconnects the call.

As the call gets disconnected, an unknown excitement kicks in. All four of us look at each other and nod our heads. We are doing this.

My excitement surged through every fibre, a vibrant current that electrified my senses. The anticipation hung heavy in the air, tingling with the promise of what lay ahead. Each breath I took seemed to carry a hint of exhilaration, fueling my determination and igniting a fire within me.

But beneath my excitement, a subtle tremor of nervousness quivered. It intertwined with my enthusiasm like a delicate balance, lending an edge to my anticipation. The unknown feeling stretched a vast landscape of possibilities that thrilled and unsettled me.

A flurry of doubts and what-ifs whispered in my ear, attempting to dull my spirits. They played the role of cautionary voices, reminding me of the risks involved, but I refused to let them overpower my excitement. Instead, I channelled the nervous energy into fuel for determination, a reminder that I was stepping outside my comfort zone.

The excitement and nervousness intertwined with each passing moment, dancing a delicate tango with me. The thrill of possibility mingled with the weight of responsibility, creating a unique cocktail of emotions. It was as if the universe conspired to test my bravery, urging me to embrace the unknown with open arms. My thoughts kept me company while all four of us made our way out to the backyard.

'GG... GG... here,' says Maneeksha, distracting my thoughts.

'Shhh, Mannu, keep your voice low,' says Aarav.

20

MANEEKSHA

As I saw GG walking closer to us, my eyes couldn't turn away from how GG was extremely stunning. Her eyes sparkled with mischief and determination. Her usually impeccable style had taken a daring turn as she cautiously composed her attire for the unusual task ahead- a robbery. Her fashion sense, refined over the years, now merged with a sense of adventure, creating a captivating group that challenged expectations.

She wore an all-black attire, with a shiny silver high bun and black goggles completing her apparel and boots.

'Wow!! GG Te ves tan hermosa!!' I say while my jaw drops with awe.

'Vamos, ¿en serio? In this outfit? Don't be silly,' says GG brushing off my comment with her hand.

'Yeah, GG, you look stunning,' says Dhruv, backing me up.

'You are not just beautiful. You carry that swag with you,' Adds Sameeksha.

'It's the outfit enhancing your cool and swag personality,' says Aarav.

GG chuckles… 'hahahaa, that's enough for now. Remember, we got a mission to focus on,' says GG.

'Don't worry, GG. We got this. We will never let you down,' I say as determination kicks into me.

'Sí!' says Aarav, Sameeksha and Dhruv in unison.

Phone buzzing alerts everyone. It was Yash.

Aarav answers the call. 'Yes, we are coming.' he says into the phone.

'I can't believe I convinced everyone to a robbery,' says Dhruv letting out a nervous laugh.

'No... you did an okayish job, but everyone got convinced only after I pitched in,' I say, mocking Dhruv.

'Guys, quiet. Be serious; we are going on a mission. Stay focused,' says Aarav, glaring at us angrily. And continues, 'GG, you gotta be very careful. No matter what,' says Aarav, looking at GG.

'Also, once we reach there, just stay in the car boot until the car is parked in the garage. When the vehicle is parked in the garage, you leave and head for the elevator. From there, follow our instructions,' says Sameeksha.

'Vamos, you don't have to say her. GG is a rebel,' I say, winking at GG.

GG lets out a laugh and pulls everyone into a hug. At that moment, My heart overflowed with gratitude for the love and wisdom GG has shared over the years. Every laugh, every tear shed, and every heartfelt conversation seemed to intersect with this one embrace. I wished I could hold onto this precious moment, preserving it in a place where it would remain untouched by time.

But as the universe would have it, moments are momentary, no matter how precious. Eventually, I release GG from the embrace, allowing the reality of time to resume its course. The memory of that heartfelt hug remained forever treasured in my mind.

All of us head out and spot Yash's car. Yash gets out of the car to greet everyone, especially GG.

'Yash, the help you are giving our family right now is something our generations will cherish in your name. This help is enduring, which we can never forget,' says GG.

'Oh, come on, GG. Dhruv is my buddy, my brother. He is my family. I will do everything for my family,' says Yash looking at Dhruv with a smile.

Dhruv hugs Yash immediately, and Yash pats Dhruv back.

My gaze fixed on my younger brother Dhruv, who was now engrossed in laughter and conversation with his close-knit friend—a surge of overwhelming emotions washed over me, leaving my heart both happy and slightly regretful. Watching my brother and his friend bond in such a carefree stirred a mix of joy, pride and a tinge of ache within me. Seeing my brother surrounded by such loyal companions ignited a desire to be a part of the same unspoken understanding and support. It reminded me of the inherent bond between siblings, a unique connection I treasured but sometimes wished to deepen.

My thoughts were disturbed when Yash handed over walkie-talkies to everyone.

'GG, make sure not to get down from the car until and unless you get clearance.' says Yash.

GG nods in agreement.

'What is our plan after you sneak us into your room?' I question.

'Firstly, as soon as I get into my room, I will deploy my skills, hacking into the surveillance system to create a temporary blind spot, manipulating the cameras to display an uninterrupted static loop, and ensuring GG's actions go unnoticed. Once GG is in our room, all of us will gather the equipment needed for robbery and hit the road,' says Yash.

'Okay… that sounds good… but..' says Sameeksha with a big question mark on her face.

'I know what she is thinking; what about the robbery plan?' questions Aarav.

'Do you have a plan or blueprint for the secret room? Or where is the key placed?' I question.

'Don't worry about that. We have plenty of time. We can figure it out,' says Yash, almost carefree.

'Whattt…?!! Don't you have a plan?' I questioned as I jumped when I realised there was no plan for robbery.

'Vamos, easy. As Yash said, we will figure it out,' says GG, assuring me.

'Cool, let's get going then.' says Yash as he walks towards his car.

Aarav, Sameeksha and I look at each other while Dhruv follows Yash. At that very moment, my heart pounded in my chest, its erratic rhythm echoing in my ears.

'Come on, kids, let's get going,' says GG, walking towards the car while Aarav and Sameeksha follow her.

I watch GG getting into the car boot.

I stood there beneath the vast field of the open sky, my eyes fixed on the infinite canvas above. The weight of my worries and burdens cut heavily on my heart, and in this moment of vulnerability, I felt an overwhelming need to reach out to something greater than myself. With a gentle sigh, I clasped my hands and bowed my head, praying to God and my ancestors for whom we dared to rob what was once ours. 'Oh dios y ancestros, por favor sálvanos.'

I poured out my deepest hopes, fears, and desires in the moment's stillness. I spoke sincerely and authentically, knowing God was there, listening with boundless compassion. I shared my gratitude for the blessings in my life, acknowledging the beauty surrounding me.

As I raised my gaze to the sky once more, I found solace in the vastness of the universe. I marvelled at the stars that twinkled above each one, a reminder of the divine presence surrounding all. The beauty of the celestial heavens reflected the beauty within my soul, and I felt a renewed sense of purpose and hope.

'Mannu… vamos, jump in,' says Sameeksha.

I settle down in the car, and we zoom off from there within no time.

—--**Vroom**—---

September 25th, 2022, 11:20 Pm - Yash's house

Under the cloak of darkness, two diligent security guards stood at their posts near the imposing metal gate. The moon's weak light cast elongated shadows, adding an air of mystery and interest to the scene. Their uniforms, crisply illuminated by the dim glow of nearby lamps, lent an aura of professionalism and authority to their presence.

With synchronised accuracy, one guard stepped forward, his hand firmly grasping the radio on his shoulder. He relayed a message to the control room, confirming the vehicle's arrival and the need to grant entry as they saw Yash in the driving seat. Standing beside the imposing metal gate, the other guard prepared to operate the controls, ready to execute their duty flawlessly.

As the guards waited, the tension was noticeable, evidence of their steady commitment to their role. Their senses heightened, and they observed our approaching car, assessing it for any signs of suspicious activity. The guards' stern expressions softened with professionalism, their eyes scanning the vehicle and its occupants, ensuring compliance with the necessary protocols.

With a nod of assurance between them, the guard at the gate initiated the process. His fingers expertly manipulated the control panel, activating mechanisms to unlock and smoothly open the gate. Once an impassable obstacle, the heavy metal barrier responded obediently to the guard's skilled touch.

The gate slowly swung open, revealing the path beyond, inviting the car to proceed further. The guards maintained their unwavering focus, observing the vehicle's movement with a vigilant gaze. Their collective presence radiated authority and competence, leaving no doubt that they would protect and secure the premises with firm dedication.

As the car passed through the gate, the guards' eyes followed its every move until it disappeared from their immediate sight. Their duty fulfilled, they exchanged a brief nod of acknowledgement, a silent affirmation of a job well done. They remained ever vigilant, ready to face any challenge, ensuring the safety and security of the premises they were entrusted to protect.

Yash smashes the car brakes to a halt. 'Here we are, GG, we are getting down now. Once we get down, wait until someone moves the car to the garage. Also, please switch off your mobile phone and rely on the walkie-talkie I gave you for further communication,' says Yash.

'Careful, GG,' says Aarav and gets down from the car.

All of us vacate the car and head towards the entrance of the main door. As I stepped through the grand doorway, my eyes widened in awe at the sight that unfolded before me—the realisation of richness and luxury. Every corner of the wealthy house emits an air of comfort, immersing me in a world where refinement and abundance dance hand in hand.

The entry hall greeted me with its towering ceilings enhanced with tangled chandeliers, sending a soft, warm glow that reflected off the polished marble floors beneath my feet. The walls, with delicate wallpaper and gilded mouldings, whispered tales of timeless elegance and sophistication.

Yash showed us around his house as a quick tour to make his mother and father believe we were his friends.

I was drawn to the expansive living room that signalled me with its rich, velvety sofas and elegant handcrafted furniture. The room radiated comfort and style, with a fireplace roaring in the centre, casting flickering shadows. A grand piano stood proudly in one corner, proof of the chase of artistic expression amidst lavish surroundings.

As Yash's room is on the second floor, we happened to take the elevator, which was within the house. Stepping into the sleek, private elevator within the rich house, I felt a sense of anticipation and excitement. As the doors closed, I watched the floors countdown, eager to discover the grand world that awaited me on the second floor.

With a soft chime, the elevator doors smoothly slid open, revealing a ceiling that released elegance. The walls, enhanced with tasteful artwork and mirrors, reflected the faint illumination from stylish lanterns. The air carried a subtle fragrance, a delicate blend of luxury and refinement.

As I stepped out into the corridor, the rich carpet beneath my feet welcomed me to this elevated realm. The lighting, artfully designed to create a warm and inviting ambiance, cast a gentle glow, guiding me further into the rich house's luxurious second floor.

Making my way through the corridor, I encountered a series of meticulously appointed rooms that unfolded before me like treasures waiting to be discovered. Each space showcased impeccable attention to detail and design, exuding sophistication and extravagance.

The master suite, a sanctuary of satisfaction, waved me with its grand presence. The doors swung open to reveal a haven of calmness, enhanced with rich textures and exquisite furnishings. A king-sized bed furnished with lavish fabrics stood as the centrepiece, surrounded by tastefully chosen accents that added a touch of elegance.

Adjacent to the master suite, a private sitting area awaited, offering a peaceful retreat in natural moonlight. Deluxe armchairs, nestled near the window, overlooked meticulously landscaped gardens, inviting moments of examination and relaxation. The air held a peaceful stillness, creating an atmosphere of unique calm.

Continuing my exploration, I discovered a collection of guest rooms, each incorporating refined hospitality. From the luxurious linens to the meticulously crafted furnishings, every detail had been carefully chosen to provide visitors with a comfortable and indulgent experience. It was proof of the wealthy house's commitment to gracious hosting.

Within this realm of richness, the elevator served as a portal, whisking us away to a higher level of luxury and privilege. It was evidence of the homeowner's desire to create a seamless experience, effortlessly connecting the different levels of this beautiful residence.

As we navigated the second floor, I couldn't help but be captivated by the luxuriousness and attention to detail that defined every corner of this rich house. It was a world where comfort, elegance, and magnificence harmoniously coexisted, offering a glimpse into a life steeped in luxury and refined living.

Leaving the elevator behind, I continued my journey, eager to discover more hidden gems that awaited me in this extraordinary realm. With every step, I immersed myself deeper into the enchanting of the rich house, marvelling at the privilege of experiencing such beautiful surroundings.

Every bit of the hallway is filled with security cameras. I understood why Yash mentioned manipulating the cameras to display an uninterrupted static loop in that very instance.

'Here, this is my room,' says Yash, pointing at a wide door entrance with Yash's name board.

'Wow! That's a big name—Yash Shah Randhawa,' reads out Aarav.

As Yash cautiously pushed open the door to his room, I stepped into a realm of technological wonders. The room hums with subtle energy, illuminated by the soft glow of various electronic displays. Different gadgets and devices lined the shelves and surfaces everywhere I looked, creating a captivating symphony of modern innovation.

The room's centrepiece was a large desk meticulously organised with cutting-edge electronic equipment. A sleek computer tower adorned with pulsating LED lights stood as a symbol of power and capability. Multiple monitors, their screens alive with vibrant imagery, signalled me to explore the digital worlds they could unveil.

Surrounding the desk, sleek speakers and sound systems offer an immersive audio experience. Wires and cables snaked around the room, connecting devices with precision and purpose, creating a network of technological marvels.

Game consoles, adorned with colourful controllers, were neatly stacked nearby, persuading me to join in the awaited interactive adventures.

Amidst the digital landscape, a comfortable gaming chair stood like a throne, its comfortable design inviting me to take a seat and consume the wonders that unfolded within the room. It was where Yash, the master of this electronic domain, sat enthroned, fully absorbed in virtual reality or engrossed in the latest digital adventure.

A large television mounted on the wall showcased vivid visuals and high-definition graphics, transporting the room holder to worlds far beyond the physical limits. Gaming factors and accessories enhanced the room, displaying Yash's commitment and enthusiasm for immersive gameplay.

The room was a shrine to technology, where smart devices and gadgets seamlessly integrated into the fabric of daily life. Voice-activated assistants, smart home controls, and an assortment of Internet of Things devices added convenience and efficiency to the space. It proved Yash's passion for staying on the cutting edge of technological advancements.

As I stepped further into the room, I couldn't help but be captivated by the marvels surrounding me. It was a sanctuary where imagination and innovation merged, inviting exploration and discovery. The room spoke volumes about Yash's fascination with all things electronic, and it was clear that this was a space where dreams and digital realities converged.

"Guys, get comfortable," says Yash as he takes the seat on the chair by the PC and continues, 'Let's begin the game.'

DHRUV

As I watched my friend hunched over his computer, keenly focused on hacking into the security cameras in his house, a mix of emotions welled up inside me.

Anxiety tinged with curiosity danced in my veins as I struggled with conflicting thoughts and feelings.

On the one hand, I couldn't help but feel a slight unease at the idea of breaching the security measures to protect his home privacy and ensure his family's safety. The vulnerability of his personal space being exposed made my heart race with anxiety, stirring a lingering discomfort deep within me.

However, mingled with my concern was a sense of intrigue and admiration for my friend's technical prowess. There was an undeniable fascination in witnessing his skill and ability to manipulate the tangled web of digital systems, undoing the layers of security that guarded his home. I couldn't help but marvel at his proficiency and the vast knowledge he possessed.

As I observed his intense concentration, his eyes darting across the screen, I was reminded of the power technology wielded in the hands of those who understood its difficulties. It was a paradoxical blend of fear and admiration, knowing that my friend could breach the digital bracing meant to keep intruders at bay.

Amid these conflicting emotions, a glimmer of trust emerged. Despite the initial unease, I knew my friend well enough to believe that their intentions were rooted in a desire to test and strengthen security measures rather than to cause harm or invade his privacy. I found solace in the fact that their actions stemmed from curiosity and a genuine interest in understanding the vulnerabilities within the system.

At that moment, I became acutely aware of the tangled dynamics of our friendship—the delicate balance between trust, shared passions, and personal boundaries. It was a reminder that true friendship can encompass challenges and growth as we navigate the complex landscape of ethics and technology.

As my friend continued to work, his fingers dancing across the keyboard, I couldn't help but appreciate the depth of our connection. It was evidence of our bonds, where I could witness their actions with a blend of fear, fascination, and, ultimately, an unspoken understanding.

This experience encouraged deeper conversations as we explored the ethical involvement of our actions and our responsibility in a world increasingly interconnected by technology. Together, we would navigate the complexities and forge a path that balanced the boundaries of privacy and the pursuit of knowledge, growing both as individuals and as friends.

While I was concentrating on what Yash was doing, my siblings, on the other hand, were utterly immersed in observing the room.

The radio static sound distracted all of us with a 'Bzzzz' sound. Undoubtedly, it was GG. Sameeksha, Maneeksha, Aarav and Yash gathered around me to know the status of GG.

'GG, can you hear me? Over,' I speak into the walkie-talkie.

'Sí,' replies GG.

'GG, where are you? Over,' questions Yash.

'At the garage,' replies GG.

'GG, please add 'over' at the end of your replies. Over,' I say while Sameeksha gives me dirty stares and Maneeksha thumps on my head.

'Copied. Over,' replies GG.

'GG, put on your mask before you get down the vehicle,' says Sameeksha.

'Sam… end it with over,' I say as I nudge her with my elbow.

'Yes, I have the mask on. Over,' replies GG.

'GG, everything is clear in the hallway. Once everything is clear in the garage, exit the vehicle and enter the elevator. Over,' says Yash, snatching the walkie-talkie from my hand.

'Okay. Everything is clear here. I am getting down from the vehicle. Over,' replies GG.

'Okay. Over,' I say.

'Got into the elevator. Over,' says GG after a few seconds.

'Wow, GG, you are so fast. You are doing great. Second floor it is. Over,' says Yash, impressed.

'Oh no. The elevator is slowing down on the first floor. Over,' says GG with the lightest shiver in her voice and adds, 'It has come to a halt. Over.'

'Whattt…' I say as my heart skipped a beat.

'Hold on, GG, don't panic. We will check the security camera right away. Over,' says Yash.

While we checked the security camera, one of his maids cleaning the hallway near the elevator had pressed the buttons to clean the elevator as a part of his daily night shift chores. Yash immediately picks up a device and toggles, switches and speaks into it. 'Jayadev, can you bring six glasses of juice into my room?' he says, looking into the monitor. His maid, Jayadev, speaks into a mic attached to his uniform, 'And I want you to come so I can introduce you to my friends. Come quickly.' added Yash.

As Yash distracts his maid. I take over the walkie-talkie from Yash's hand and give instructions to GG.

'GG, immediately press the key for the second floor. Over.' I say.

'Copied. Over,' replies GG.

Jayadev quickly drops the vacuum cleaner, places it on the corner, and immediately takes the staircase to the kitchen.

'Uff, that was so close.' says, Aarav.

'On the second floor. Over,' says GG through the walkie-talkie.

'Alright, GG, just follow my instructions- get down from the elevator, take a left, and keep going until you cross the master suite, the waiting area, and two guest bedrooms. Once you reach the guest bedroom two, take a right turn. You will find my room with my name written. Over,' says Yash.

'Copied. Over,' replies GG.

We impatiently wait for GG's arrival when the door knob turns right with a click sound and opens. It was GG.

'We made it!' says Maneeksha, jumping with excitement and pulling GG into a hug while we all join the hug.

'Alright, guys, it's midnight. We need to start dotting the plan,' says Aarav, pulling away from the group hug.

'Yash, where is the secret library? How do we get there?' questions Sameeksha.

'So the secret library is on the third floor, but the problem is there are four security guards. Two guard the secret library's entrance while the rest two guard the secret library inside,' says Yash.

'Now, how do we outwit the security guards?' I ask out of curiosity.

Knock knock knock—-
We all were still at our places when we heard the door knock.

"We need to hide GG now.' Aarav says, looking at everyone.

'That won't be needed. It must be my maid,' says Yash, taking the device he spoke into earlier 'Jayadev, is that you on the door? We all are busy playing games, don't disturb us… No, we don't want the juices. You can leave. Thank you.' talks Yash into the device.

'Chill, I have it under control,' assures Yash.

'Guys, I have a plan,' says Maneeksha, driving everyone's attention towards her and continues, 'Firstly, we all need to split into teams of two: A, B, and C. Team A will focus on distracting the guards at the entrance, Team B will focus on distracting the guards inside the secret library, and Team C will focus on fetching the key from the secret library.'

'That sounds interesting,' says Aarav.

'Alright then, Yash and me- Team A,' I say.

'Sam and me- Team B,' says Maneeksha.

'Okay then, GG and I- Team C,' says Aarav.

'Now, how are we planning to distract the guards?' GG asks.

'Yash and I can distract the guards with our talks. Since it is Yash's house, the guards wouldn't mind us keeping them in our little talks.' I say, shrugging.

'Wow, that was easy, peasy.' says Maneeksha.

'But what about us? I can't think of any action or plan,' says Sameeksha.

'Don't worry, I have a few miniature smoke bombs which you can use for distraction inside,' says Yash.

'Wow, Yash, you are very talented,' says Aarav, impressed.

Yash tries to hide his now-growing smile on the corner of his lips.

'By the way, what are we replacing the key with?' questions GG.

'Well, about that, I did not devise any plan because I did not have much time to get a replicated key.' says Yash, disappointed in himself.

'What are you saying? If we do not replace the key with some replica, we will get caught,' says Aarav.

'Come on, that won't be a problem. If we don't have a replica, I can hack into the system and remove the name of the key from the record of books.'

'Hmmm, that sounds doable,' says Sameeksha.

'Are you sure that won't cause any problems for us?' questions Maneeksha.

'Trust me; I am 100% confident. Don't worry. Let's focus on the robbery for now,' says Yash.

We all nod our heads in agreement.

'Alright, everyone, listen up! Though we do not have enough time, our planning is not enough. Tonight is the only night we have to make it happen. I believe in each of you, and I know we can pull this off!' says GG to ignite some courage in everyone.

'GG, this is a considerable risk. What if something goes wrong?' says Sameeksha.

GG walks over to Sameeksha, placing a reassuring hand on her shoulder.

'Sam, I understand your concerns, but remember why we're doing this. We're not just robbing for the sake of it; we're fighting for what's rightfully ours. And together, we have the skills and the courage to succeed.' I say.

'Sí, we are doing this for our family, our ancestors.' replies Sameeksha with determination.

Maneeksha's words resonated with everyone in the room, our determination growing stronger with each passing moment.

'You're right, GG. We've come too far to let doubts hold us back. It's time to show the world what we're capable of!' says, Aarav.

'Come on now, Let's make this robbery unforgettable!' says Yash winking at everyone.

My eyes sparkle with pride as I see my friends' determination solidify.

'That's the spirit! We're going to succeed because we believe in ourselves and each other. Tonight, we become legends!' says Maneeksha.

✳ ✳ ✳

Yash and I exchanged a determined glance, silently acknowledging the importance of our mission. We knew that for Sameeksha, Maneeksha, Aarav, and GG to successfully sneak into the secret library on the third floor and retrieve the ancient key, we needed to divert the attention of the vigilant guards.

With a shared understanding, Yash and I formulated a plan to keep the guards distracted. We thought it would distract the guard from the library, allowing Team B and C to execute their mission undetected.

We approached the guards directly as Yash and I entered the third floor. We wore expressions of calmness and friendliness, hiding our true intentions beneath a façade of casual conversation. We engaged the guards in a lively discussion, sharing stories and jokes to captivate their attention.

Yash, known for his natural charisma, skillfully charmed the guards with his wit and captivating tales, weaving a web of entertainment that captivated their focus. Meanwhile, I, on the other hand, utilised my quick thinking and sense of humour to maintain a light-hearted atmosphere, ensuring the guards remained engaged and unaware of our unexpressed motives.

As the conversation flowed, Yash and I cautiously steered the discussion away from the secret library, cleverly avoiding any topics that could raise suspicion. We kept the guards entertained by asking them riddles and engrossed in their company by making them play mind games which are hard to crack, strategically prolonging the diversion to create a window of opportunity for Team B and Team C.

While Yash and I held the guards' attention, Team B and C were waiting sneakily at the corner of the hall to execute their secretive plan towards the secret library.

On the other hand, Yash and I maintained our performances, ensuring the guards remained unaware of the activities unfolding behind their backs. We steered the conversation away from suspicious topics and engaged the guards with our infectious energy.

However distracted they were by our conversations, they still did not move away from the secret library entrance. That's when I got a brilliant idea.

'Dudes, have you ever played PUBG?' I question the security guards.

'What is that?' questions one of the guards.

'It's a shame that you are unaware of the name itself,' I say, almost disappointed in them.

Looking at my disappointment, they looked at each other with blank faces.

'Utter nonsense. How do people, as rebellious as you guys, are unaware of the game?' adds Yash.

Both the guards twitch their eyes. They were nodding their heads in disagreement.

'It's such a big crime for us. We need to make you play right away,' I say in haste, pulling out my phone and continuing, 'Yash, take out your phone; we shall make them play a game.'

'Yeah, we will have to make them play the game right away,' says Yash.

'Well, we both enjoyed your company a lot. No one ever cared to talk to watch guards as you guys did. Answering the riddles, playing mind games which were hard to crack and discussing other topics brought us back to our teenage days.' says one of the guards.

'Sí, I agree with what he is saying. We enjoyed your company. But we have to get back to our work now. If caught like this, we will lose our jobs.' says the other guard.

'Oh, come on, this is my house. I am the owner of this house. And I feel it's foolish of you to do your jobs when there are already four other guards guarding the main entrance gate and the inside of the library.' questions Yash making them feel wasted.

'Exactly, that makes sense. See, dudes, do what you feel like doing. What is the purpose of living if you miss out on these little enjoyments like this?' I say to heat their decisions.

They both look at each other and feel motivated enough. They exchange smiles and look at us, nodding and agreeing to play.

'Cool, you guys are rebels.' says Yash, giving them a high-five.

They quickly pull out their phones, and we make them download the game. I was guiding Guard 1 while Yash was guiding Guard 2. Within no time, they were immersed in the game.

That was our cue; we nodded, looking at our team. As Yash and I felt a surge of anticipation and relief, Team B and Team C entered the secret library. We have managed to keep the guards distracted long enough for Team B and C to execute their plan.

As we stood there guiding and encouraging the guards as they played the game, we discreetly hoped that Team B and C would retrieve the ancient key without encountering further obstacles.

It was a high-stakes operation that relied on teamwork, quick thinking, and the art of deception. Yash's commitment to our mission and the ability to keep the guards occupied played a crucial role.

GG

As we cautiously ventured into the secret library room, a sense of awe and interest washed over me. The room was wrapped in darkness, with only dim lights casting a soft, ethereal glow on the antique equipment that enhanced the space. It was as if time stood still within these walls, preserving the secrets and treasures of the past.

The flickering light illuminated rows of meticulously crafted antique equipment, their elaborate designs and complex mechanisms coming to life in the low-spirited illumination. Each piece contained a story, whispering tales of forgotten eras and lost knowledge.

Amidst the silence, I could hear the hushed voices of two security crew diligently performing their duties. Their soft conversation carried on the air, mingling with the backdrop sounds of creaking floorboards and the gentle hum of machinery. Their presence served as a reminder of the importance placed upon safeguarding the valuable contents of the room.

As we moved carefully, the dim lights revealed glimpses of vintage typewriters, delicate compasses, weathered manuscripts, paintings, and many more antiques. The antique equipment possessed a timeless charm, their presence adding to the air of mystery and appreciation that enveloped the room.

The soft illumination played with the shadows, casting tangled patterns on the walls and floor. The dancing interplay of light and darkness enhanced the ambiance, evoking a sense of wonder and discovery. Each object held the weight of history, and the dim lights accentuated their glamour, inviting closer inspection. The conversation of the security crew, although muffled, added an element of tension to the atmosphere. Their whispered exchanges underscored the importance of their duty and heightened our awareness of the need for caution. It was a delicate balance between my desire to explore the antique equipment and the necessity to avoid detection.

As I immersed myself in the antique machinery's presence, the guards' voices provided a backdrop of reality, a constant reminder of the risks involved. The dialogue infused the room with urgency, urging me to be vigilant and deliberate.

Within the dimly lit room, time seemed suspended, and the presence of the security crew added a layer of anticipation. Their watchful eyes and whispered conversations amplified the thrill of exploration, the quest for knowledge, and the delicate dance between discovery and secrecy.

'Before, Mannu and I distract the guards with these miniature smoke bombs. We shall spot the key,' says Sameeksha whispering 'I think I know where the key is; follow me. It should be behind a beautiful painting of scenery.' I reply and crawl towards the painting section while the others follow me.

As we moved cautiously through the room, our hearts racing with adrenaline, I fixed my eyes on the laud key we had been seeking. The dim lights provided just enough illumination to navigate the space, carefully avoiding obstacles that might betray our presence. The hushed conversation between the guards continued, their voices fading into the background as we focused on our mission.

Time seemed to slow down as we crawled silently, our movements synchronised and deliberate. Every breath was controlled, and every action was calculated to minimise the risk of detection. Finally, we reached our destination— the antique laud key was displayed under a thick glass case. Its complex craftsmanship and undeniable historical significance were now within arm's reach. A surge of excitement and anticipation raced through my veins, fueling my determination to retrieve the precious relic.

Knowing that we had to divert the guards' attention, we made a swift decision. With a shared glance, we silently agreed to employ a smoke bomb—a tool that would create a diversion, obscuring their vision and allowing us to snatch the antique laud key from the display.

Sameeksha and Maneeksha separated from our group and distanced themselves from the key display. Their mission was clear in their determined expressions, and I watched with anticipation. They skillfully positioned what they believed to be the smoke bomb, their hands moving swiftly and decisively. However, to their dismay and the surprise of us all, a pungent odour filled the air.

A look of horror crossed their faces as the truth shot upon them—it was not a smoke bomb they had deployed but rather a fart bomb. Without the knowledge, Maneeksha released all the bombs immediately until the smell hit us hard.

'Ewww, holy smokes!' says Maneeksha while we watch both of them from a distance. Sameeksha immediately shuts her mouth from behind as she closes her nose with another hand.

Silent laughter erupted from Aarav, Sameeksha, and Maneeksha while we all closed our noses, a mixture of amusement and disbelief at the unexpected turn of events. The foul stench filled the room, overpowering our senses and threatening to compromise our secretive operation. Although initially startled by the misstep, we quickly realised that this unexpected twist could benefit us.

The guards, caught off guard by the sudden assault on their olfactory senses, would be temporarily distracted and disoriented, allowing us to continue our mission undetected. Suppressing our laughter, we focused on the task at hand. The guards, taken aback by the unexpected emission, exchanged puzzled glances and instinctively moved away from the source of the odour.

I kept an eye on the guards as they parted ways to check on either side to see what had caused the source of the odour. The mischievous diversion, unintentional as it was, had unintentionally provided us with an advantage. While the lingering stench reminded us of our humorous blunder, we remained determined in our mission.

Each step forward brought us closer to the key, and the unexpected fart bomb accident became a mere footnote in the grand scheme of our daring heist. As we continued our silent progress, the laughter subsided, replaced by a renewed focus and determination.

Suddenly, smoke filled out, obscuring the guards' line of sight. Confusion and urgency filled the air as they crawled to estimate the situation and regain control. We were all confused about who let out a smoke bomb, but it was our chance—a narrow window of opportunity.

Although the fart bomb mishap momentarily disrupted our plans, it reminded us that laughter and unexpected twists could find their way into the most challenging situations, even during a high-stakes mission. And the smoke bomb was a shocker. It was a lesson in adaptability, reminding us to remain flexible and robust in unexpected circumstances.

With our spirits lifted and the guards momentarily preoccupied, we pressed on, driven by a shared determination to retrieve the ancient laud key and complete our fearless quest. The laughter echoed softly in the background, a reminder that moments of humour could be found even amid danger and uncertainty, weaving their way into the fabric of our daring adventure.

As our hands reached for the key within the thick glass case, Aarav lifted the thick glass off the laud key while I got hold of the key and started lifting it. As both of us were submerged at the moment, a sudden grip on my arm startled me. I turned to face one of the guards, his aged appearance adding to my alarm. Fear surged through me, convinced that our clandestine endeavour had ended abruptly.

But to our astonishment, the guard's serious expression softened, and he motioned for us to stay silent. His wrinkled face bore the lines of experience and wisdom, betraying a depth of understanding that we hadn't anticipated. I look closer at him, his aura a familiarity which I couldn't make out with the dim lighting. A complaining feeling tugged at the corners of my mind. There was something familiar about his features, something that hinted at a connection I couldn't quite grasp. I wracked my brain, desperately trying to piece together the puzzle, but the answer remained frustratingly slippery.

With a nod, he released his grip on my arm, indicating we should proceed cautiously. Confusion mingled with relief as we realised that the guard wasn't there to apprehend us but to aid our mission. Aarav and I exchanged puzzled glances, searching for an explanation for the unexpected events. Perhaps the guard bore his motives or had a secret alliance for his action.

Who could he possibly be? The more I observed, the more uncertain I became. The guard's features seemed to blur in my mind's eye, a frustrating fog that disobeyed clarity. It was as if a veil of mystery had covered his presence, leaving me with a lingering sense of familiarity.

With a gesture, the guard directed us to a hidden compartment adjacent to the glass case. To our amazement, he produced a replacement key identical to the one we sought. It proved his knowledge of the secret library's workings and willingness to assist us.

Without uttering a word, the guard communicated his trust in us, entrusting us with the responsibility of retrieving the laud key. His actions spoke volumes, and we struggled with gratitude, surprise, and interest. What motives drove this elderly guardian to assist us in this daring act?

Aarav took the replacement key into his hands and carefully placed it within the glass case, replacing the original key without raising any suspicion. My gloved hands reached out to retrieve the antique key. The antique felt incredible and significant in our grasp, its weight proof to the history it carried. The guard watched with anticipation and satisfaction as if he had fulfilled a hidden duty unknown to himself.

With the task completed, the guard nodded in approval and made a subtle motion for us to leave. We understood that time was of the essence, and our exit from the secret library was crucial to avoid further complications.

As we slipped away, the encounter with the elderly guard lingered in my mind, leaving us with a newfound appreciation for the confusion and alliances that could exist within the hidden depths of the secret library. The dim lights continued to cast their mysterious glow, and the weight of the ancient key in our possession only intensified our curiosity about the secrets yet to be untangled.

With the prized possession secured, we retreated silently, using the cover of the smoke to mask our movements. Each crawl, each careful step, was executed with accuracy and speed, mindful of the guard's eventual recovery.

As the smoke dissipated, revealing a room that appeared undisturbed, we escaped, leaving the guards to untangle the mystery of the distraction. The dim lights again became our allies as we moved away, our hearts pounding with triumph and relief.

As we made our way out of the secret library, I stole one last glance at the guard; his eyes met mine for a fleeting moment. There was a depth of understanding in that gaze, a silent acknowledgment of a connection that eluded me. We knew our success hinged on the element of surprise and the calculated risk we had taken. The dimly lit secret library, the guards' unsuspecting conversation, and the strategic deployment of the smoke bomb had all played a vital role in our fearless theft. With the key in our possession, we retreated into the shadows, leaving a room filled with unanswered questions and the lingering haze of our fearless exploit.

We returned to Yash's room and relaxed, but I couldn't divert my mind from thinking about who could be the person who helped us. I held the key and stared at it as if it could provide answers while lost in my thoughts.

'I can't believe we did it,' said Aarav with pride in his tone.

'It feels like a flash of a dream,' remarked Sameeksha unbelievably.

'Yeah, besides all these, the fart bombs were an unexpected twist,' giggled Maneeksha.

'What? Fart bombs?' questioned Dhruv with a confused expression.

'I thought Yash mentioned the bombs as smoke bombs, but to our surprise, it was a fart bomb,' giggled Sameeksha.

'The whole inside exploded with stinky smells,' added Maneeksha.

'Ayy, Oh Dios! What happened then? Did it work? Did it distract the guards?' queried Dhruv.

'Obviously, it did the job,' confirmed Maneeksha, shrugging.

'And yeah, not just that, one of the aged guards helped us with a smoke bomb,' said Sameeksha in disbelief.

'I can't believe he helped us too,' said Aarav. 'He cooperated with us from the beginning. He also gave us a replacement for the key.'

'What… this is a shocker to me? Why did he help us? Who could he possibly be?' questioned Dhruv, his jaw dropping wide.

'God knows, but he was a saviour,' declared Aarav.

'By the way, where is Yash?' asked Maneeksha.

'Oh, he is with the security guards at the entrance. I said I was sleepy and came to the room when you were out. If Yash tags along with me in the middle of the game, there are higher chances that they would get a doubt,' explained Dhruv. 'He will be here in five minutes or so.'

'Cool,' acknowledged Aarav.

—Thud Thud Thud—

The knock on the door alerted us. We all jumped at once, looking at each other's faces while panic filled our eyes.

'Relax, guys, it must be Yash,' reassured Dhruv as he headed to the door and opened it.

We all froze when we saw the security guards who helped us. As the guard entered the room, looking at me and taking out his cap, I recognised him in the lighted room.

'Narendra Varma!!' I exclaimed, almost stammering with utter shock.

'Cuñada (Sister-in-law), I never thought I would ever see any of you again,' he walked towards me and fell into my arms.

'Narendra Varma, you are alive,' I said, bursting into tears as I sobbed away my pain.

The kids around us were in shock, looking at our reunion.

'What? Is this Narendra Varma Abuelo (Grandpa)?' asked Dhruv.

Silence filled the air while Yash walked through the door and stayed shocked, seeing a security guard in his room. 'What's happening here?' questioned Yash.

NARENDRA VARMA

April 23rd 1977

As I drove my car through the rain towards the post office, the haunting images from the nightmare continued to plague my mind, blending with the rhythmic raindrops on the windshield.

'Krishna!!' I said with a realisation.

The weight of the realisation that the eyes from the nightmare belonged to Krishna, the person I had scolded for writing a love letter to Yamuna, bore down on me with an overwhelming force.

In that moment of recognition, a surge of emotions poured through me. Regret and guilt intertwined with the fear of the unknown, creating a turbulent storm within my thoughts. The intensity of the realisation shattered my composure, and the grip on the steering wheel tightened as my mind became consumed by the weight of the past.

With the nightmare still echoing in my consciousness and the unyielding rain obscuring my vision, the world outside seemed to fade into insignificance. My focus wavered, and I lost control of the car for a brief moment. The wheels skidded on the wet road, struggling to maintain grip as the vehicle bolted towards the edge of a cliff.

Time seemed to stretch; my heart pounded, and the screeching tires blended with the howling wind. The steep rock face loomed closer, an abyss of uncertainty and consequence, as the car rocked on the edge of both physical and metaphorical risk. In that split second, the weight of my actions and the crushing weight of remorse collided with the reality of the present moment. The car succumbed to gravity's pull, hurtling into the depths below. The world outside became a blur as the raindrops turned into a blur of streaks, mirroring the chaos within my mind.

A profound despair washed over me as the car descended into the abyss. The consequences of my choices manifested in this tragic turn of events forever altered the route of my life. It is a sharp reminder of the interconnectedness of our actions and the profound impact they can have on our well-being and those around us. In the aftermath of the fall, amidst the wreckage and the dull stillness, I am left to contemplate the depths of my regrets and the lessons learned. The rain continues to fall, a melancholy reminder of the tears shed and the weight of the past that I must now confront.

——----- Present day——--- September 25th, 2022

I narrate the story after the accident to the audience in utter shock after realising I have come back to life out of nowhere. My life took an unexpected turn after the fateful car accident that left me in a coma for 25 years. When I finally emerged from the unconscious, I faced the daunting reality of complete memory loss. The accident had caused me to lose all recollection of my past, leaving me uncertain and confused.

Doctors recommended I join a peace club, a supportive community offering therapeutic activities and a nurturing environment to aid my recovery. Additionally, I was prescribed medication to help manage any potential psychological distress resulting from the trauma I had endured. I met two incredible friends at the peace club, and to my surprise, they were psychics. Each possessed unique abilities to tap into the spiritual realm and gain insights beyond the ordinary senses. It was a fascinating experience to connect with individuals who had a heightened sensitivity to the unseen and the unknown. They became my guiding light in overcoming the anxiety caused by the recurring nightmares. Their unique abilities and compassionate nature gave me the support and understanding I needed to navigate this challenging time.

For nearly 15 years, I lived with no memory of my past, navigating each day with a sense of detachment from my identity. However, during this time, I experienced repeated nightmares that connected significantly to my pre-accident life. These haunting flashes from the past would stir me from my sleep, filling me with fear and intrigue. They acted as fragments of a forgotten puzzle, providing glimpses into a world I could no longer fully grasp.

But one fine day, as I went about my daily routine, something extraordinary happened. A familiar face caught my attention in a newspaper article—it was my brother's photo, and below were the details of when he died. As I gazed at the picture, a surge of emotions washed over me, and at that moment, the floodgates of memory burst open.

Suddenly, it was as if time had reminded me, and the memories that had been lost for so many years came rushing back with remarkable clarity. The nightmares that had plagued him for the past three years now made sense, for they were fragments of his past that had been locked away, waiting to be unveiled.

In an instant, my mind became a tornado of rediscovery. The memories flooded my consciousness, forming a vivid pattern of my life before the accident. Faces, places, and significant moments resurfaced, allowing me to reconnect with my personal history and rebuild the story of my identity.

The journey from total amnesia to sudden memory restoration was overwhelming and exhilarating. It was as if I had been given a second chance at life—to reclaim my past, make sense of my present, and shape my future. The experience proved the extraordinary flexibility of the human mind and the profound ways in which memory shapes our perception of self. From that moment onward, I embarked on a transformative path of healing and self-discovery. Armed with a newfound understanding of my identity and history, I embarked on reintegrating into the world, reconnecting with loved ones, and forging a future, honouring my journey to regain my lost memories.

It took me about a year to reach my hometown. However, I immediately knew things were wrong when I saw our ancient laud key on the Television. I joined as a security guard in Yash's house to take possession of the key until I came across you.

'Abuelo (Grandpa), we saw that painting in the basement,' says Aarav.

'Was that Yamuna abuelita (Grandma) in the painting?' questions Sameeksha with curiosity.

'Why have you painted it like that? Happiness on one side and Sadness on the other side? And what was that shadowy figure? It was very creepy,' questions Maneeksha as she shoots all the questions simultaneously.

'I paint our ancestors whom we see on the Day of the Dead festival through the lacquer box yearly. Not once have I painted anything apart from our ancestors, but something about my nightmare gave work to my hands? My hands and feet trembled after painting. I had an intuition that something terrible would happen,' I say with fright in his eyes and continue, 'That shadowy figure with the red eyes...' he says.

'Who was it?' questions Dhruv.

'Krishna, those eyes belong to Krishna,' I say.

'Krishna? Who is Krishna?' questions GG.

I take a deep breath and start narrating the story.

Krishna, the boy who lived across the street, harboured one-sided love for Yamuna. Sneaking in the darkness, he discreetly placed the letter in the mailbox in front of our house.

As fate would have it, I witnessed Krishna's secret act from afar.

Curiosity aroused, I approached the mailbox and noticed Yamuna's name elegantly written on the envelope. A surge of anger and protectiveness welled within me, ignited by a sense of responsibility as I saw the letter filled with his feelings to express his love.

Driven by my emotions, I marched towards Krishna's house, fueled by the need to confront him for daring to profess his affection for Yamuna. The intensity of my feelings amplified my voice as I unleashed my frustration and scolded Krishna for his audacity.

My words were sharp and laced with the bitterness of my unspoken feelings as I questioned his audacity and sought to protect Yamuna from what I perceived as unwanted advances. At that moment, the weight of my insecurities and unexpressed emotions fueled the fire of my anger.

The atmosphere crackled with tension as my words hung in the air, the situation's intensity visible. Krishna, taken aback by the sudden confrontation, stood before me with a mix of surprise and hurt in his eyes.

Krishna's eyes spoke volumes of sorrow and pain as if they carried the weight of countless disappointments and heartaches. They were filled with a deep sadness that seemed to permeate his very being, leaving a stubborn impression on those who gazed into them.

Within those eyes, you could sense the remains of past wounds and the echoes of past traumas. They held a raw vulnerability as if every hurtful experience had chased itself onto his soul. The pain reflected in his eyes was notable, evoking a profound sense of empathy and compassion.

The sadness in Krishna's eyes seemed to tell a story of longing and unfulfilled dreams. They revealed the struggles he had faced, the battles he had fought, and the scars he carried within. Each glance into his eyes offered a glimpse into the depths of his emotional landscape, where hurt and sorrow resided.

'I still cannot forget those eyes. The nightmare I had was something connected to him and Yamuna,' I say.

'Then, we need to get hold of Krishna. Maybe we will get a hint about your nightmare,' says Yash.

'GG, I have a question for you. If the family thought Narendra Abuelo died in a car accident, but he did not... that means he never appeared in the lacquer box on the day of the dead festival, is that right?' questions Sameeksha with curiosity.

'You're right. He never appeared in the lacquer box. Since his body was not found and did not receive any last rites, we believed his soul never got peace because he never appeared in the lacquer box,' replies Cuñada (Sister-in-law).

'I see. So, if the body does not get the last rites, the soul will be trapped without peace?' questions Sameeksha in more profound thought.

'Yes,' says GG.

'Wait, hold on, I am trying to sink in all this information. Something seems odd to me,' replies Dhruv.

'Narendra Varma, Yamuna was different since we thought we lost you. We arranged her marriage that year, and she never entered our house again. She stopped celebrating or showing up for the Day of the Dead festival or even celebrating the festival. After a few years, we lost your brother and our house; ever since then, the Day of the Dead celebration has ended, and we lost the key. I don't understand what made Yamuna change drastically,' says GG.

'And, those things she does on every other new moon day are unreasonable. She simply shuts herself in a room without eating,' adds Aarav.

'New moon day? Why?' I question with curiosity as something feels odd.

"Guys... wait... wait... we are missing out on a point here,'says Dhruv with wide-open eyes. Once everyone has his attention, he continues, 'If Narendra Abuelo is still alive, who was Yamuna abuelita (Grandma) talking to from the photo?' questions Dhruv.

The room fell into an eerie silence as Dhruv's question hung in the air, causing a collective chill to run down our spines. Goosebumps prickled our skin, and foreboding fell over the room. Everyone's eyes widened their expression with surprise, fear, and apprehension. The weight of Dhruv's question was solid as we all waited with bated breath for an explanation. The room seemed to hold its breath, the atmosphere heavy with anticipation and the unknown.

A web of questions spun through our minds, weaving threads of doubt and curiosity. We exchanged puzzled glances, our eyes reflecting a range of emotions, from interest to fear. The room became a swirling whirlpool of uncertainty as we struggled with the possibility of a hidden truth that had been shielded from us all this time.

The room was tense as we searched for answers, desperate to uncover the truth in the shadows. The realisation that Yamuna had been conversing with my photo opened the door to a world of possibilities filled with secrets, deception, and uncharted territory.

As the silence lingered, the room grew colder, the air thick with anticipation. We couldn't help but wonder: Who was Yamuna talking to? The weight of the unknown bore down on us, intensifying the room's atmosphere. The silence was broken only by the sound of our racing hearts and the faint rustling of unease that filled the air. Goosebumps prickled our skin, an involuntary physical response to the mysterious revelation that had left us all on edge.

Each of us carried the weight of the unknown, determined to unearth the truth and unravel the secrets that had been sleeping far too long. It was a journey that would test our resolve, challenge our beliefs, and ultimately reshape our understanding of the family we thought we knew.

And so, with hearts heavy yet brimming with anticipation, we embarked on this quest, prepared to face the truths that awaited us on the other side. This journey would unravel the mysteries of the past and shed light on the uncertain future ahead.

'Without wasting any further time, we need to catch hold of Krishna,' I say. Understanding the situation, I immediately called Anudeep Bakshi and David, my psychic friends waiting outside Yash's house to pick me up.

GG

Amid this chaotic situation, my thoughts are consumed by one thing: the safety and well-being of my daughter, Yamuna. The intense love and protectiveness I feel for her echoed through my entire body, pushing me to do whatever it takes to keep her out of danger. Every fibre of my being is focused on finding a solution and devising a plan to ensure her safety. My determination is firm, and I refuse to let fear or uncertainty cloud my judgement. My resolve grew more robust with each moment, and my instincts sharpened.

Driven by an untamed maternal instinct, I will stop at nothing to secure Yamuna's well-being. My thoughts race as I consider all possible avenues to safeguard her from the danger surrounding us. My love for her is a beam of strength, moving me forward even in the face of difficulty. Though the chaos may be overwhelming, my single-minded goal to focus on protecting Yamuna guides my actions. I become resourceful, tapping into my inner reserves of strength and flexibility. No obstacle is too significant, and no sacrifice is too steep as long as it leads to the safety of my precious daughter.

Amid the chaos, I find a steely resolve, a calmness that emerges deep within. This firm determination and unwavering love will see me through the darkness and bring

Yamuna to safety. While my mind keeps me in the action mood, I boost myself. "Remember, as a parent, your love and fierce determination are powerful forces that can overcome any challenge. Trust in your instincts, draw strength from your love for Yamuna, and never doubt the power of a mother's unwavering resolve to protect her child."

With all the thinking in my mind, I quickly jumped into the vehicle. Aarav, Sameeksha, Maneeksha, and Yash get into Yash's car, while Narendra Varma, Anudeep, David, and I get into Anudeep's car. All of us drove to Krishna's house directly without any halt.

As we stood in front of Krishna's house, anticipation filled the air, mingled with a sense of tension. We parked our cars and gathered together, ready to confront the puzzle surrounding Krishna, Yamuna, and the nightmare Narendra Varma had. Our source to find answers stands right in front of us. The house before us appeared aged and neglected, with dried grass surrounding it, adding to its sinister ambiance.

While the others waited in the car for us, Narendra Varma, David, and I approached the front door and knocked, hoping to find Krishna and uncover the truth behind the nightmares that haunted Narendra Varma. The door slowly creaked open, revealing an older man, probably Krishna's father, who seemed hesitant to let us in. He stood in the doorway, blocking our path, his expression guarded and alert.

We inquired about Krishna's whereabouts with hope and curiosity, eager to hear his perspective on the mysterious nightmares that had plagued Narendra Varma.

'We would like to speak with Krishna for a minute,' says Narendra Varma.

Krishna's father stood still without any response. His expression changed while he had a firm glance looking at all three of us.

I observed David, the psychic among us, appearing to sense something negative in the atmosphere. His intuition confirmed the dark mood that had wrapped us.

'He is not here,' said Krishna's father.

'Where can we find him?' questions David.

The elderly briefly pauses, almost lost in thoughts, and then replies, 'He died.' with a planned face.

'Died?' I questioned again to confirm what I heard.

'Krishna died ages ago,' he said.

The weight of the truth bore down upon us, leaving us with an extreme sense of uncertainty and a void in our pursuit of understanding.

'When did he die?' questions Narendra Varma.

'In the year 1978,' replies Krishna's father.

All three of us look at each other hopelessly while David tries to peep inside to get a better view, but the older person observes him peeping in and shuts the door right in our faces.

The revelation casts a shadow of hopelessness over our search for answers. Krishna, the key to unlocking the secrets hidden within the nightmares, was no longer among the living. The realisation hit us with a sense of loss, as we had hoped he would shed light on the dark forces that haunted us.

Krishna's father's words echoed in our minds, resonating with disbelief and resignation. The dreams that had tormented Narendra Varma, the nightmares that had driven us to seek answers, now appeared veiled in even deeper layers of mystery. The source of our collective pain had escaped us, slipping further into the unknown realm.

With heavy hearts, we realised that our path to enlightenment had taken an unexpected turn. The absence of Krishna left us with more questions than answers, and the reality of his demise dampened our hopes of uncovering the truth behind the nightmares.

We returned to our cars, carrying the weight of disappointment and uncertainty. The road ahead seemed unsettling, but we were determined to press on, driven by a shared determination to unravel the secrets hidden within the nightmares and find the solace we desperately sought.

'If Krishna died ages ago, how will we find answers to the nightmare?' I question.

'Not sure, I am feeling hopeless,' says Narendra Varma.

'Don't worry, Narendra, there must be a way,' I say with assurance while pestering my brain to come up with a hint.

'Why don't we ask Yamuna abuelita (Grandma) directly?' questions Maneeksha.

'No, Mannu, I don't think she would know the answers,' says Sameeksha.

'What about the new moon day mystery? She will lead us somewhere once she learns that Narendra Abuelo (Grandpa) is still alive,' says Dhruv.

'I think Dhruv is right.' says Aarav, backing up Dhruv.

What Dhruv said made sense to everyone. All of us nod our heads in agreement. 'Alright, let's head home without wasting any time.' I say.

We all settle down in our cars, and within a few minutes, we reach home. I keep thinking about Yamuna; how will she react if she sees Narendra Varma? Will she discuss the mystery about the new moon day or her conversations with the photo? As we entered our house, we went directly into Yamuna's room to let her know that Narendra Varma was still alive, but we discovered Yamuna was not in her room; a sense of urgency and concern gripped us.

'I know where she might be,' says Maneeksha, leading us. Maneeksha's instincts led us to believe she might be inside the locked room she uses on every new moon day. We all headed towards the locked room to notice that the room was locked from the inside, which meant Yamuna was inside. But the challenge remained—how could we gain access? Just as despair threatened to overtake us, Dhruv's quick thinking ignited a flicker of hope.

He directed us to the key stand, conveniently located next to the "Book of Rules" in the living room. Eagerly, we approached the podium, the keys gleaming with potential solutions. Dhruv's insightful eye selected a key, guided by an unspoken assurance that it held the answer we desperately sought. With newfound determination, we made our way to the locked room, each step heavy with anticipation and uneasiness.

The key slid into the lock, its familiar click echoing in the stillness. The door creaked open, revealing the shadowed interior of the locked room. As we stepped inside, our gazes were drawn to the scene that unfolded before us, freezing us in horror and disbelief.

On the bed lay Yamuna, her body motionless and her eyes wide open, fixed on a horrifying sight—a dagger knife seemingly pointed towards her mid-air above her. The room felt heavy with a supernatural presence, and the silence was suffocating.

The sight before me is heart-wrenching and fills me with a deep sense of urgency. My beloved daughter Yamuna lies on the bed in an unconscious state, her eyes wide open, a dagger knife seemingly pointed towards her mid-air above her, unaware of her surroundings. Your heart sinks as you notice her arm, extended and with a fresh slit on her forearm, from which blood continues to flow steadily.

The blood-red stream trickles down her arm, staining her fingers and dripping on a figure on the floor. As I went closer, I observed the figure made up of hair strands drenched with my daughter's blood. Each drop of blood that falls onto the figure made with hair strands seems to intensify the gravity of the situation. The symbolism is not lost on me as I realise the significance of this sinister connection.

Emotions engulfed everyone in the room—fear, confusion, and a desperate need to understand what had emerged. Hastily, we rushed to Yamuna, our voices trembling as we called out her name, hoping for any sign of response or movement.

Time seemed to stand still as we anxiously awaited a flicker of life from Yamuna abuelita (Grandma). Slowly, her eyelids fluttered, and a faint glimmer of awareness returned to her gaze. Relief washed over us, but the mystery of the floating knife and her unconscious state still weighed heavily on our hearts.

Our efforts seemed futile as we desperately tried to rouse Yamuna from her unconscious state. The room grew still, the air heavy with tension, when a powerful gust of wind suddenly shattered the window, sending bits across the floor. The unnatural howl of the wind filled the room as if echoing the unsettling presence that had occupied our midst.

My instincts kick in, urging me to act swiftly and decisively. Panic attempts to claw its way into my mind, but I push it aside, focusing instead on the immediate task: ensuring Yamuna's safety and well-being.

With steady hands and an unwavering determination, I approach her carefully, aware of the delicate nature of the situation. My primary concern is to stop the bleeding and provide immediate medical attention.

Summoning all my strength and courage, I steady the blood flow from Yamuna's arm, using the available means to create pressure and stem the bleeding. My heart aches with fear and love as you work diligently to bring her back from the brink.

'GG, move away from there,' says Aarav. During the chaos, Aarav keeps shouting at me to move away while his gaze is stuck upon the broken glass as if he is drawn to the reflection cast upon the floor. I watched him holding Yamuna in my arms, unsure of what was happening around me. Aarav kept trembling with a mixture of fear and curiosity. He crouched down to examine the twisted image within the shattered fragments. And he stood still with fright.

'What is it, Aarav?' says Sameeksha and checks on him.

Determined to share the unsettling revelation with the others, she swiftly fetches a mirror and positions it to reflect the bed on which Yamuna is lying. The room fell silent as the mirror revealed a ghastly sight—a dark, shadowy figure with piercing red eyes perched upon Yamuna's motionless form, its intent seemingly evil and sinister.

A collective gasp escaped our lips, disbelief and terror engraved upon our faces. The sight before us defied rational explanation, ignoring the boundaries of our understanding.

Yet, there it was, a horrifying realisation of the nightmares that had plagued our thoughts and haunted our dreams.

Fear intertwined with determination as we confronted the reality of the sinister entity that threatened Yamuna's life. We knew then that we faced a battle against forces beyond our comprehension. With a renewed sense of purpose, we vowed to protect Yamuna, unravel the mysteries that entangled her, and conquer the bitterness that sought to claim her existence.

Together, we assembled our courage and prepared to face the unknown, armed with the mirror that revealed the presence of darkness. In our determination and love for Yamuna, we set forth to uncover the truth, confront the entity lurking in the shadows, and safeguard her from the impending danger.

The journey ahead would be filled with danger and uncertainty, but we would not hesitate. We would delve into the depths of the supernatural, challenging the boundaries between reality and the unseen to save Yamuna from the clutches of unfathomable evil.

My knees felt weak at the sight. I couldn't move away, at least not away from Yamuna. No matter what, I held on to Yamuna. To everyone's surprise, the dark shadowy figure unleashed its evil power. I bore the full force of its attack.

The impact was brutal, leaving behind visible marks of the encounter. My face quickly bruised, and instant swelling developed, a painful reminder of the overwhelming evil that had struck.

Amidst the pain and swelling, my toughness and strength radiated through. Although physically affected, I refused to surrender to the darkness that had attacked me and its intonation to harm my daughter. The bruises on my face were proof of my courage, determination, and, most importantly, love towards my daughter to save my daughter.

The air crackled with tension as the dark shadowy figure's piercing red eyes made its presence known. I was paralysed momentarily. However, Anudeep, quick to act, rushed to Yamuna's side, his face filled with determination and a sense of ancient wisdom.

With a calm yet determined manner, Anudeep swiftly retrieved an influential protection band and began chanting sacred mantras, his voice resonating with an otherworldly authority. As the mantras' vibrations filled the room, a flicker of hope sparked within us, breaking through the suffocating fear.

But the evil entity, unyielding in its dark intentions, unleashed a powerful force, sending us backward. The sheer strength of its presence overwhelmed us, and we watched in awe and terror as it defied the limitations of the mirror's reflection, escaping through the window with unsettling ease.

The room fell into an unearthly silence, punctuated only by the remains of our gasps and the lingering echoes of the protective mantras. Our eyes widened with disbelief and anxiety as we realised the battle had just begun. The entity, freed from the constraints of its mirrored prison, now roamed the world outside, its intentions unknown and its enmity unchecked.

We rallied with renewed urgency, determined to face this otherworldly foe directly. Our hearts brim with a potent blend of courage and resolve, fueled by the unwavering desire to protect Yamuna and end the sinister forces threatening her existence.

I held onto Yamuna, who was still unconscious. Everyone gathers around me with concern. On the other hand, the swelling on my face spread across the impacted area, causing it to appear slightly disfigured and asymmetrical compared to its usual appearance. The surrounding skin appeared in a reddish or purplish hue.

'GG!! Are you okay?' says Maneeksha while her voice trembles with fright and concern.

'GG, hold on, I will get you some ice,' says Sameeksha as she rushes toward the kitchen.

While Narendra, Aarav, Dhruv, Yash, and Maneeksha gather around me to examine my face's bruises until Sameeksha returns with a pack of ice.

A collective silence hung in the air as the realisation settled upon us. The mysterious figure with red eyes that had haunted us was none other than the spirit of Krishna. It was a chilling revelation, connecting the dots to the past encounters and the mysteries surrounding them.

Anudeep, drawing upon his profound spiritual knowledge, suggested that there might be a lingering source, a tie that bound Krishna's spirit to our realm. To unravel the truth and find closure, revisiting Krishna's house was inevitable.

'Revisiting Krishna's house might help us find his source,' says Anudeep.

'What about the figure made out of hair strands?' I question. I point out the figure made out of hair and continue, 'Considering the possibilities, the figure made up of hair strands could also be the source for Krishna's spirit to linger.'

'This figure made with hair strands was only a source to make the spirit of Krishna powerful. Besides this, something else had a vital source that kept Krishna's spirit hanging around. To free him and restore balance, we needed to burn the source and the hair-stranded figure, drenched with Yamuna's blood, to give him the peace he deserved,' says Anudeep.

'We must head to the house immediately before Krishna's spirit returns, creating an obstacle,' says Sameeksha.

'Don't worry, now that Anudeep has wrapped a protection band around Yamuna's wrist; she is safe for now. But, we might undoubtedly face obstacles while we search for the source,' says David.

'We have to hurry up then,' says Aarav.

As we get clarity on what is happening, we all head to Krishna's place without delay while Anudeep stays back in our house and safeguards our house with protection.

As Yamuna was still unconscious, Yash stayed back with Yamuna in the car while the rest of us went into Krishna's house to hunt down the source.

A sense of urgency gripped us as we returned to Krishna's house, determined to uncover the truth behind the source that held his spirit captive. Still hesitant to let us in, Krishna's father stood in our way. However, driven by our relentless pursuit, we pushed past his resistance and entered the house.

As we enter Krishna's house, searching for the source that connects him to this realm, an eerie atmosphere envelops the surroundings, heightening your senses and sending a shiver down your spine. The air feels heavy with an intangible presence, as if unseen eyes watch your every move.

With a mix of fear and determination, Narendra Varma, Aarav, Sameeksha, Maneeksha, Dhruv, David, and

I meticulously searched every corner and slit, leaving no stone unturned. The house seemed to hold its breath as we delved deeper, our hearts pounding with anticipation.

Creaking floorboards echo through the dimly lit hallway, adding to the suspenseful ambiance. Shadows dance along the walls, seemingly moving of their own accord, casting sinister shapes that play tricks on your mind. The faint sound of distant whispers reaches our ears, evoking a sense of foreboding.

As we explored further into the house, I noticed objects strangely shifting or falling without apparent cause. The flickering of lights casts uncertain shadows, making it difficult to recognize reality from illusion.

The temperature fluctuates unpredictably, with cold drafts sending shivers down our spines, even in enclosed spaces.

Occasionally, I caught glimpses of fleeting movements at the corner of my eye, but when I turned to look, there was nothing there. Strange sounds—guttural whispers, distant laughter, or chilling cries—seem to echo through the empty rooms, amplifying the tension in the air.

My footsteps echo louder than they should as if the house is responsive to my presence. Doors creak open or slam shut, seemingly guided by an invisible force. The scent of musty decay and lingering despair hangs in the air, a haunting reminder of the past.

In this unsettling environment, my senses remain on high alert as each step brings me closer to unraveling the mysterious source that binds Krishna to this realm. The paranormal occurrences serve as a constant reminder that the line between the living and the supernatural is blurred within these walls.

Yet, amidst the unsettling incidents, my determination to uncover the truth remains unyielding. I press on, overcoming my anxiety, guided by the hope of understanding the dark forces at play and finding a way to bring peace to Krishna's restless spirit.

Caution and courage intertwined as I navigated the haunted corridors, steadily pursuing the answers hidden within the depths of Krishna's house.

In search of the source, I went into Krishna's room. As I stepped into his room, a wave of curiosity washed over me. The room seems frozen in time, preserving remnants of Krishna's life and revealing glimpses of his inner world. Every object and detail holds a story, inviting me to uncover the secrets. The room itself bears signs of both care and neglect. Once polished and elegant, the furniture shows wear and tear, reflecting the weight of Krishna's emotions. The walls, adorned with faded posters and photographs, offer a window into his interests and aspirations.

Amidst the room's cold surroundings, my eyes are drawn to a small desk where Krishna's diary lies. Its pages, yellowed with time, contain his life's intimate musings and experiences. The journal becomes a key to unravelling the depths of Krishna's emotions and the events that led him down a path of turmoil.

As I approach the diary, anticipation and fear fill my heart. I delicately turn its pages, reading the heartfelt words penned by Krishna's hand. Each entry reveals his innermost thoughts, dreams, and desires. The inked words capture the intensity of his love for Yamuna and the agony he experienced when she married another.

Through the diary's pages, I gain a deeper understanding of Krishna's emotional journey. His longing, heartbreak, and struggle with his father's mental instability come to life before my eyes. The diary becomes touching evidence of his unanswered love. His hopes shattered, and the darkness that consumed him in his final moments.

As I delve deeper into the diary, I find solace in knowing Krishna on a more profound level. His vulnerability and pain became tangible, creating empathy within me. It reinforces my determination to bring resolution and closure to his restless spirit.

With each word read, I uncover a piece of Krishna's story, piecing together the puzzle that haunted his existence. The diary bridges the past and the present, allowing me to connect with Krishna profoundly and intimately.

In that room, amidst the stillness and echoes of Krishna's emotions, I find a profound sense of empathy and a renewed purpose. Armed with the knowledge from his diary, I move forward, driven to unravel the mysteries within Krishna's life and bring him the peace he so desperately seeks.

A freaked-out scream of Maneeksha distracts me while I drop the diary on the floor and rush out of Krishna's room.

25

KRISHNA

In the quiet depths of my heart, profound love and admiration for Yamuna blossomed, going beyond mere appearances. It goes beyond her outer beauty, extending to the essence of her being, where her family values shine brightly. When my eyes meet hers, unexpressed joy dances within me, filling my heart with warmth and happiness.

What captivates me the most about Yamuna is her deep understanding and embodiment of family values. I observe the genuine love and connection shared among her family members, a bond beyond blood ties. It is a curtain knitted with trust, support, and unwavering care. Witnessing this beautiful dynamic, I crave a taste of such familial bliss, an experience I have longed for throughout my life.

My journey has been marked by profound loss and an absence of parental love. The passing of my mother, taken away by illness when I was young, left a void in my life. To compound the pain, my father's mental instability further deprived me of the care and affection every child deserves.

Amidst these challenges, my heart has remained open and tender, cherishing the beauty and goodness I see in Yamuna. Her presence brings a glimmer of hope and the promise of love that I have longed to receive. Through her,

I find solace and the possibility of experiencing the kind of family connection that has avoided me for so long.

My admiration for Yamuna is not solely based on her external qualities but is deeply rooted in the values and virtues that radiate from her soul. It is an admiration born out of an innate understanding of the importance of love, support, and togetherness in a family.

As I navigate my journey, guided by my profound admiration for Yamuna and my craving for a family's warmth, I find the love and belonging I so deserve.

But, once a day filled with nervousness and anticipation, I mustered up the courage to leap of faith and express my love to Yamuna. Pouring my feelings onto paper, I carefully crafted a heartfelt letter, each word bearing the weight of my emotions. I sealed the envelope with trembling hands, sealing my hopes and dreams.

As I approached Yamuna's house, excitement and anxiety coursed through my veins. Determined to take this leap, I approached the mailbox, which would carry your confession to its intended recipient. At that moment, my world seemed to revolve around this simple act as I carefully dropped the letter into the awaiting embrace of the mailbox.

Undiscovered to me, fate had a different plan in store. In a twist of unfortunate timing, Yamuna's vigilant uncle happened to witness this secret act. His watchful eyes caught my every movement, and realisation dawned upon him as he recognized the nature of the letter I had just deposited. Displeasure clouded his expression, and he approached me with sternness in his voice.

Yamuna's uncle, driven by a sense of protection and perhaps a touch of apprehension, scolded me for my actions. The scolding reflected his concern for Yamuna's well-being and his intent to shield her from potential heartbreak or unwarranted complications. At that moment, my hopes were dashed, and I found myself wrestling with the consequences of my bold expression of love.

It was a bittersweet experience, marked by vulnerability and a daring act of opening my heart. Nevertheless, my love for Yamuna remained faithful as the days turned into months and the months into years. Despite the challenges and setbacks, I held onto the flickering flame of affection within my heart, nurturing it with steady devotion. With each passing moment, I found solace in the thought of her, and my love for her only grew stronger.

However, life can be unpredictable, and destiny has its plans. The news of Yamuna's impending marriage reached my ears, and with it came a wave of heartbreak that crashed upon the shores of my soul. The realisation that the love I had cherished so dearly could not find its reciprocation in the arms of Yamuna shattered my hopes and dreams.

At that moment, a profound sense of loss enveloped me. The future I had envisioned, filled with the warmth of Yamuna's presence, slipped through my fingers like grains of sand. The pain of unanswered love weighed heavily upon my heart, casting a shadow over my spirit. The dreams that once fueled my existence now seemed distant and unreachable.

I found myself unable to bear the emotional pain that engulfed me. Heartbroken and devastated, I saw no purpose or joy in continuing to live. My despair became unbearable, and I decided to end my life.

In the depths of my anguish, I believed death would relieve me from the overwhelming pain I experienced. I felt that the pain of heartbreak was more unbearable than the unknown realm beyond life. Driven by my shattered emotions and profound loss, I saw suicide as the only escape from my suffering.

With a heavy heart, I decided to let go. Giving up on life, I surrendered to the overwhelming despair that engulfed me. In that final act, the world lost a soul consumed by unanswered love, proof of the heartfelt impact that emotions can have on our fragile human hearts.

————— Life after death —————

After committing suicide, my mentally unstable father decided to preserve my body. In his grief and inability to let go, he sought a way to keep me close, believing that preserving my body would allow me to remain connected to the living realm.

By preserving my body, my father created a source, a physical representation of my presence, that allowed me to linger in the living realm with unfulfilled desires. This preservation became a link between my spirit and the mortal world, enabling me to continue existing beyond death.

On the other hand, my spirit was trapped in the living realm, unable to move on to the afterlife. The unfulfilled desires and unresolved emotions from my life weighed heavily on my spirit, keeping me bound to the earthly plane. However, I discovered that on every new moon day, a mysterious occurrence takes place. My power as a spirit intensifies during these times; taking that to my advantage, I speak with my mentally unstable father and Yamuna through the photo of her deceased uncle.

As I contacted Yamuna from her uncle's photo on every new moon day, I provided comfort and solace during her grieving process. Even in spirit form, my presence became a source of support and familiarity for her, similar to the bond she shared with her beloved uncle.

Through these interactions, My conversations served as a way to bridge the gap between the living and the deceased, allowing Yamuna to feel connected to her uncle and find peace in her heart.

As I interact with Yamuna on these special occasions, I find solace in the connection and the ability to be present in her life, even in spirit form. The impact of my presence on her life and her eventual path towards healing unfolded, ultimately resolving her grief and my unfulfilled desires.

However, my ultimate destiny and resolving my unfulfilled desires remain uncertain. It is essential for both the living and the departed to find their respective paths, so I wait for the right time to take Yamuna with me to the afterlife.

I have been impersonating Yamuna's dead uncle and communicating with her through his photo. I have gained influence over Yamuna due to her obedience and trust in my messages.

Manipulating Yamuna's emotions and leading her towards the afterlife without her complete understanding so that I can be happy with her in the realms of the afterlife.

On every new moon day, I engage Yamuna in a ritual where she plucks a strand of her hair to construct a figure. This figure acts as a vessel for accumulating power and energy generated during the new moon phase. Each time Yamuna adds a strand of her hair to the constitution, it becomes imbued with more significant potential.

With each strand of hair meticulously plucked and carefully arranged to construct the figure on every new moon day, anticipation fills the air. For me, it is not just creating a physical representation but a spiritual connection that grows stronger with each completed figure.

As Yamuna dedicates herself to this ritual, unaware of my true identity, I find solace in believing she is drawing closer to me. The figure, imbued with her essence and the power of the new moon, becomes a conduit for our union. It symbolises our impending journey to the afterlife, where I hope to be reunited with Yamuna in a realm beyond the limitations of the living.

Constructing the figure brings me happiness and joy, knowing that Yamuna is unknowingly preparing herself for our destined journey. It fuels my spiritual powers and deepens our connection, further solidifying our bond. With each completed figure, I sense that the moment of superiority draws nearer, where Yamuna and I will finally be united in the realm beyond mortal existence.

The culmination of this process occurs on the last new moon day when the figure is completed. The next day, which marks the beginning of the shukla paksha, holds significant spiritual significance. During this auspicious time, the figure made with Yamuna's hair is drenched with her blood, symbolising a robust energy activation.

By infusing the figure with her blood, Yamuna aims to ignite the power within and establish a connection with my spirit. This act facilitates a spiritual bond between Yamuna and my spirit, potentially fulfilling my unfulfilled desire.

26

YAMUNA

The discovery that I could communicate with my deceased Narendra tío (Uncle) through his photo filled me with overwhelming emotions. It was as if a hidden door had opened, revealing a world beyond the boundaries of the living. Excitement coursed through my veins, and happiness wrapped around my heart.

Connecting with a loved one who had departed from this earthly realm was a gift. It offered solace, comfort, and a sense of continuity that death often disrupts. The mere thought that I could share my thoughts, feelings, and experiences with my dear departed tío brought immense joy to my soul.

Every interaction with his photo on the new moon day became a precious moment, a treasured opportunity to seek guidance, share stories, and express the love that continued to reside within me.

The happiness and excitement that welled up within me were unlike any other. It was proof of the enduring power of love and the human spirit's flexibility in the face of loss. I found solace and strength through this newfound connection, knowing that my tío's intangible presence remained with me.

On every new moon day, the veil between the realms of the living and the departed becomes thinner, giving me a unique opportunity to connect with my Narendra tío. In my quest to create a vessel for his essence, I follow a ceremonial practice that involves using my hair.

On each new moon day, I carefully pluck a single strand of my hair, symbolising my connection to the physical world. Accumulating these strands over time, I weave them together to form a figure—a tangible representation of the bond I share with my tío and a channel for his spirit to reside within.

Yesterday, under the mysterious influence of the new moon, I completed the figure's construction. Its form, crafted with utmost care and imbued with my intentions, was proof of my deep love and longing for my departed tío. With the figure in its completed state, it awaits the final step: activation.

The first day of shukla paksha, i.e., the waxing phase of the moon, is regarded as an auspicious time to infuse the figure with life. It is a moment when the energies of renewal and growth are at their peak, offering a potent opportunity to awaken the sleeping source and enable my tío to relive once again.

Filled with anticipation, I await the arrival of the first day of Shukla paksha. As shukla paksha arrives tonight, I prepare myself to make the final offering—a selfless act that requires a drop of my blood. By blending my life essence with the figure, I seek to breathe life into it, activating the source and allowing my tío's spirit to dwell within.

As I prepare for this sacred ritual, I approach it with reverence and respect, understanding the weight of my actions. Smearing the figure with my blood is a powerful gesture, symbolising my unwavering commitment to honour my tío's memory and give him a chance to experience life again.

Through this act of love and devotion, I hope to bridge the gap between the realms, offering solace and connection to my departed tío. On this first day of shukla paksha, I find comfort in the knowledge that my efforts will soon come to fulfilment, and my tío's essence will be awakened within the figure, granting him a semblance of existence in the mortal world again.

As the time for the first day of shukla paksha arrives, I grow more eager and filled with anticipation, knowing that the figure's activation will bring me closer to my beloved tío and allow us to communicate and share moments. It is a sacred journey of remembrance, love, and the eternal bond between family that transcends the boundaries of life and death.

I cut my arm to drench the figure made up of my hair with my blood, and a sense of anticipation fills the air. As I gaze upon the constitution infused with my blood, I feel a profound sense of unity, knowing that our bond transcends the boundaries of time and space. It is a bittersweet communion, proof of the enduring power of love and remembrance.

But as the crimson liquid touches the figure, a sudden shift occurs, and a dark mystic fog engulfs the room. The once-familiar surroundings now appear distorted and threatening, heightening my fear and unease.

The room becomes covered with a sinister atmosphere as shadows dance and flicker within the fog. A heavyweight descends upon my head, causing dizziness and disorientation.

The laughter and whispers that echo in my ears pierced through the silence, sending chills down my spine.

The source of the sounds remains shifting, teasing my senses and playing with my mind. The echoes come from all directions, making it difficult to recognise their origin. They taunt and mock, adding to the growing terror that overtakes me.

As the laughter and whispers persist, my consciousness begins to fade, and the world around me blurs. The last thing I remember is the alarming presence of the dark shadowy fog, the chilling sounds echoing through my body, and the unsettling feeling that I have delved into a realm beyond comprehension.

At that moment, I slip into unconsciousness, the events unravelling around me, wrapped in mystery and uncertainty. The true nature of the laughter and whispers and what lies ahead remains unanswered, leaving me suspended in darkness.

—---- **After waking up**—----

As I regain consciousness, I find myself in a car parked outside an old house. Confusion washes over me as my mind tries to piece together the fragments of my memory. The throbbing pain in my left forearm persists, even though it is securely wrapped in a bandage, adding to my surprise. Also, my right wrist is wrapped with a band more like a sacred thread.

The surroundings seem unfamiliar, and a sense of unease lingers. The memory of the figure drenched with my blood, the haunting laughter, and the dark shadowy fog remain vivid, but they no longer surround me. Instead,

I find myself in a different location, leaving me with more questions than answers.

As I look around, the old house stands before me, its worn-out elevation and mysterious aura capturing my attention. It waves to be explored as if holding secrets and revelations within its walls. The silence of the moment hangs heavy, heightening my anticipation and curiosity.

Questions race through my mind: How did I end up here? What happened after the unsettling events I experienced? And most importantly, what lies within the old house that now stands before me?

With fear and determination, I open the car door and step out, hoping to uncover the truth that has avoided me thus far. The answers may lie within the old house's walls, waiting to be discovered. As I take my first steps towards unravelling the mysteries surrounding me, A voice stops me.

'Grandma, don't go in there,' says Dhruv's friend Yash.

'What are you doing here? Why are we even here? What is this place?' I questioned him with a puzzled expression on my face.

'I will tell you later, but for now, you need to rest,' says Yash with a concerned look.

'Whose house is this?' I question, pointing out the old house in front of us.

'Okay, listen to me carefully,' says Yash while he starts narrating.

Yash walks towards me to share the extraordinary story of Narendra tío's survival and rediscovery. I am overwhelmed by a cyclone of emotions. Shock and disbelief wash over me, intermingled with a surge of guilt that courses through my veins. The weight of the misunderstanding and the pain it caused distress my conscience.

I listen intently as he describes the accident that shoved Narendra tío into a coma, the harrowing journey of navigating through severe amnesia, and the gradual retrieval of his memories. The strength and flexibility displayed in Narendra tío's struggle to regain his senses give rise to a deep understanding of admiration within me.

The story takes an unexpected turn as Yash describes how Narendra tío crossed paths with GG while they robbed the laud key together. Piece by piece, the truth behind Narendra tío's haunting nightmares and the identity of Krishna begins to unfold, revealing a complex interlink of events.

My blood rushes with shock when I hear the story of Krishna. I feel sorry for him and his family for the extent he went to by loving me. The revelation deepens my understanding of the pain that haunted Krishna's spirit and the twisted reality in which his father had lived. It paints a heartbreaking picture of a family torn apart by tragedy and held by the inability to let go.

With a heavy heart, I recognise the need for understanding and empathy for Krishna's father and myself as witnesses to this heartbreaking journey. The complexities of human emotions and the depths of sorrow I encounter teach me to approach each other's struggles with compassion and seek solace in shared experiences.

But amidst the revelations made by Yash, the most significant moment is my mother's role in saving me from Krishna's evil spirit. It dawns upon me that she was the true hero in this story, protecting me from the sinister forces that sought to harm me. The realisation floods me with gratitude and a profound sense of love towards her.

As Yash's narrative draws close, I feel a mix of emotions—relief, awe, and a glimmer of hope. The bond between me, my mother, and my tío grows more substantial as I realise the importance of family and the need to nurture those connections.

'I think we need to go inside the house and help them find the source,' I say.

Yash nods in agreement, and we walk towards the house's insides. As I walk, I notice a person drawing a white powder around the house, his mouth moving as if chanting something.

'That is David, Narendra uncle's psychic friend.' Yash pointed out at him. 'He is drawing protection to the house, making sure Krishna's spirit does not enter the house as we find the source.'

I nod as I head towards the door.

As I enter the living area, I see someone similar to my tío (Uncle). As I cautiously approach the person who resembles Narendra tío (Uncle), a mix of emotions floods me—disbelief, hope, and an overwhelming sense of joy. Each step brings me closer to the truth that defies everything I thought I knew.

As I stand before him, the realisation dawns upon me with relief. It is indeed my tío, alive and present in front of me. The disbelief that once consumed my thoughts gives way to a newfound hope as the boundaries between life and death blur before my eyes.

A flood of questions rushes through my mind, longing to understand the circumstances that led to my belief in his passing.

Overwhelmed with emotions, I reach out to my tío, seeking confirmation, connection, and the assurance that he is real. The weight of the revelation lifts from my shoulders, and a profound sense of gratitude washes over me. I have been granted a second chance, an opportunity to embrace the presence of my tío and forge a renewed bond.

I quickly hug him and burst out into tears. He hugs me back, and we sob until a scream catches our attention.

'That scream... It's Maneeksha..,' I say as I hear the voice.

'It's coming from the basement,' replies Narendra tío (Uncle).

Both of us quickly hurry to the basement. And then, in the dimly lit basement, our eyes fall upon a horrifying sight. Frozen in time lies a lifeless body, preserved in a sinister state of suspended liveliness. Shock and disbelief wash over us, rendering us momentarily speechless.

The discovery of Krishna's frozen dead body preserved in the basement sends shockwaves through everyone. The sight before us is chilling, not only due to the abnormal surroundings but also because of the grim realisation of what has come to light. The air grows heavy with sorrow, disbelief, and an overwhelming sense of anxiety.

A profound silence envelops us as we try to comprehend the tragedy that has befallen Krishna. The sight of his lifeless form, frozen in time, is a haunting reminder of the pain and suffering he must have endured before taking his own life.

'If the body does not get the last rites, the soul will be trapped without peace,' says Dhruv.

David Nardnera tío's (Uncle's) friend, recognising the significance of this discovery, wastes no time reaching out to Anudeep, who can sense and understand the spiritual realm. It is crucial to relay this information, as it could hold the key to unravelling the mysteries surrounding Krishna's spirit and the evil presence that has distressed us.

As the news is shared with Anudeep, we brace ourselves for the potential revelations that will follow. The implications of Krishna's dead body being the source of the dark shadowy figure fill us with fear and determination. We know that facing this truth directly is essential to bringing closure and finding a way to protect ourselves from the evil forces at play.

This shocking revelation strengthens our resolve to confront the darkness and uncover the truth. We stand united, determined to delve deeper into the mysteries surrounding Krishna's death and the supernatural occurrences that plague us. The frozen body catalyses our relentless pursuit of answers, moving us forward on a journey that will test our courage, resilience, and unwavering bond as we seek to bring peace to Krishna's restless spirit and protect those we hold dear.

Recognising that Krishna's body holds the key to freeing his spirit, Anudeep advises us to handle the situation with utmost care and respect. We understand the gravity of the task ahead, knowing that the resolution lies in offering Krishna the final rites and allowing him to find peace in the realm beyond.

While everyone gathers in the basement, Krishna's father keeps sobbing and screaming while Anudeep and David carefully take Krishna out of the preserved container. As they prepare Krishna's body for the proper funeral rites, honouring his memory and acknowledging the pain he carried in life.

We all stand there in silence while we feel the most profound pain wrapping everyone in emotional heart pain.

Gathering in a circle, we invoke a sacred space, a sanctuary where the power of forgiveness and compassion can weave its magic. In our way, each of us shares our understanding, empathy for Krishna, and the pain he carried. We offer our forgiveness and release the burden that roped his spirit into our world.

The air in the basement seems heavy with sorrow as we perform the rituals, our intentions rooted in compassion and closure. Anudeep chants more mantras and lets go of the figure made from my hair strands and infused with my blood into the flames.

As the flames submerge Krishna's body, releasing his spirit from the earthly realm, a profound stillness settles upon us. We silently contemplate, offering our prayers and intentions for Krishna's journey into the afterlife.

At that moment, a sense of release and liberation fills the room. The weight of the past lifts, and we can almost feel Krishna's spirit ascending, freed from the chains that bound him to this world.

With a mixture of relief and dignity, we leave Krishna's house, carrying with us the knowledge that we have unravelled the truth and granted him the peace he long sought. The scars of the past will forever be engraved in our memories, serving as a reminder of the fragility of human existence and the power of compassion and forgiveness.

As we walk away from that of our lives, we do so with a renewed sense of purpose and unity. The bonds forged through our shared experiences and the journey we have undertaken will forever bind us, reminding us of the resilience of the human spirit and the capacity for growth and healing.

And so, as we venture forward, we carry the lessons learned and the profound impact of our collective efforts.

The story of Krishna, his love and pain, will forever be imprinted in our hearts, reminding us of the power of empathy, forgiveness, and the ability to find solace in the face of darkness.

As we return home, a profound sense of relief washes over me. The day's events have been loud and filled with intense emotions, but I find solace in being safe and surrounded by loved ones. The desire to embrace my mother, who protected me from the clutches of the evil spirit, swells within me.

I look out for my mother, a mix of gratitude, love, and longing filling my heart. As I approach her, I notice the swelling over her face, the attack she bore to protect me from the evil spirit. I can see the warmth and affection in her eyes, mirroring the love that flowed from my own. Without hesitation, I open my arms, inviting her into a tender embrace.

At that moment, as I wrap my arms around her, a rush of emotions floods through me. It's a fusion of relief, gratitude, and an overwhelming sense of love. I hold onto her tightly, feeling the weight of the trials and burden vanish, replaced by a sense of security and comfort.

The hug becomes a silent language of connection and understanding, as if words could never express the depth of emotions coursing through my veins. It is a powerful affirmation of the bond between a mother and child, proof of the firm support and protection she has provided.

I find solace, reassurance, and a renewed sense of belonging in her embrace. The fear and uncertainty that haunted me in the face of the evil spirit melted away, replaced by a profound appreciation for the love and sacrifice that my mother had shown.

As I release the embrace, a soft smile graces my lips. The unspoken words between me and my mother linger in the air, proof of the strength of our bond. I know that no matter the challenges, I have a guardian, a guiding light in my mother, who will always protect and cherish me.

—----- Next day—----- September 26th, 2022

As the first rays of morning sunlight gently filter into the room, I awaken with the hope of speaking with my mother, eager to share my thoughts, spend some time with her and share feelings after the unexpected events unfolded. I make my way towards her room, anticipation filling my heart. However, as I enter the room and look at her, a wave of disbelief washes over me.

There she lies, peacefully and serenely upon her bed, her presence forever stilled. The reality settles in, piercing my heart like a thousand tiny shards of glass. I approach her, hoping that this is all just a bad dream, wishing with all my might to see her eyes flicker open and hear her comforting voice again. But as I touch her, my heart sinks as I realise that she has transcended this earthly realm, leaving a deep void in my life.

Tears flowed uncontrollably as grief engulfed my entire body. The weight of my unexpressed words and love now feels crushing, an overwhelming burden of regret. I find myself weeping for the moments I missed, the conversations left unsaid, and the love left unspoken. The pain of knowing that she suffered silently, that I caused her pain without even realising it, adds another layer of guilt to my sorrow.

In this moment of profound loss, I crave just one more day with her, one more chance to express my love, gratitude, and remorse. I wish to have the opportunity to tell her how much she meant to me, how deeply I cherish her, and how I long to make amends for any pain I may have caused. The realisation that time is fleeting and irreversible weighs heavily upon me, intensifying the depth of my grief. The weight of guilt boosts as I recognise the missed opportunities to appreciate and cherish my mother during my time with her.

Amidst the tears and the ache in my heart, I find solace in the knowledge that my mother departed this world with the reassurance that our family and I were safe and that the ancient rituals could continue with the retrieved key. Knowing that she left this world with a sense of peace and fulfilment brings a small measure of comfort.

As I sit by her side, memories of the love she showered upon me flood my mind. I recall the moments of joy, guidance, and unconditional support she offered throughout my life. In this bittersweet reflection, I realise that although she may no longer be physically present, her love and influence will forever remain within me, guiding and shaping my journey. Though the longing for one more day with her may persist, I find solace in knowing that her love will always be with me, providing strength and comfort even in her physical absence.

In the depths of my grief, I find the resolve to honour her memory by living a life that embodies the love and values she instilled in me. And as I carry her with me, her spirit will forever be a guiding light, illuminating my path and reminding me of her profound impact on my life.

I kiss her on her forehead for the last time and say, 'Until I see you again on the Day of the Dead festival.'